Coast-to-coast praise for
A Visible Darkness

"Plenty here to re~~~~~~~~~~der: the rapid-fire, gritty dia-
logue and th~~~~~~~~~~~rd-living, earthy hero. Freeman'~~~~~~~~~~~~ester, a genius who stutters
~~~~~~~~~~~le, and a new love interest,
~~~~~~~~~~~ twist. . . . Satisfying fare."
                                    —*Publishers Weekly*

~~~~~~~~~~~ and criminal courts reporter in
~~~~~~~~~s that the success of his first detective
~~~~~~~~ *ae Edge of Midnight*, was no fluke. . . . Shot
th~~~~~gh with the same burgeoning suspense and rich,
brooding atmosphere. . . . King sets up a powerful parallel
between the primordial feel of the Everglades and the mean
streets of South Florida, with civilization seeming much
more cutthroat. King seems well on his way to creating a
knockout series."   —*Booklist* (starred review)

"He effectively captures the feel of swampy South Florida,
making the landscape a key element in his engaging thriller.
In much the same way James Lee Burke uses the bayous of
south Louisiana in his stories, King's Florida has a distinct,
character-revealing personality."   —*The Albany Times Union*

"Well into James Lee Burke territory, Jonathon King's second
novel featuring ex-cop turned unofficial and reluctant PI,
Max Freeman, is top class. . . . This is an author with a big future."   —*The Independent on Sunday* (London)

"It's the characters in this book that make it irresistible."
                                    —*St. Petersburg Times* (FL)

"King skillfully contrasts midcentury Florida with the early
millennium South. . . . He weaves a powerful plot into this
volatile mix, provides a credible hero and a memorable cast.
All this plus a subtle love story and some superb detective
work."   —*St. Louis Post-Dispatch*

"King writes a compelling story."   —*Rocky Mountain News*

"This excellent effort proves that there's still room for another detective in the crowded Florida fiction landscape."
                                    —*Library Journal*

"King continues to write as powerfully as in his striking
debut."   —*Kirkus Reviews*

continued . . .

"With his first novel, King jumps into James W. Hall territory and lands firmly on his feet. . . . The author's stylish prose and insider's knowledge of the sinuous, dangerous Everglades give [it] a fresh twist . . . King uses descriptions of places and environment to reveal character and attitude, much as Hall, James Lee Burke, and Robert B. Parker do. . . . Skillful writing, original characters, and evocative settings initiate a welcome new series." —*Publishers Weekly* (starred review)

"Takes us far deeper into the Everglades and much closer to the hard-core survivalists. . . . [Freeman] turns into an impressive action hero." —*The New York Times Book Review*

"The atmosphere is as thick as the humid summer nights in Jonathon King's evocative first crime novel. . . . Often lyrical prose. . . . A talented writer, one who obviously knows the territory." —*South Florida Sun-Sentinel*

"A nail-biting thriller that will place King near the apex of 2002 crime fiction. . . . Pages turn swiftly . . . keeps readers on the tangy edge until the end. . . . A bracing tale about a tormented man's private redemption, with tenuous twists and turns through the bayou." —*Coral Gables Gazette*

"Stylish, suspenseful, and well-paced, this book is a welcome change from the gross-'em-out school of crime writing favored by too many local practitioners of the genre these days. Mr. King is an author to watch." —*Miami Today*

"This might be Jonathon King's first novel but it definitely won't be his last. He has developed a character who . . . is a heroic figure, trying to do the right thing even if he ends up in trouble because of it. Readers will love *The Blue Edge of Midnight* because of the complexity of the plot and the exciting finale." —*Midwest Book Review*

Also by Jonathon King

The Blue Edge of Midnight

A VISIBLE DARKNESS

JONATHON KING

AN ONYX BOOK

ONYX
Published by New American Library, a division of
Penguin Group (USA) Inc., 375 Hudson Street, New York, New York 10014, U.S.A.
Penguin Books Ltd, 80 Strand, London WC2R 0RL, England
Penguin Books Australia Ltd, 250 Camberwell Road,
Camberwell, Victoria 3124, Australia
Penguin Books Canada Ltd, 10 Alcorn Avenue,
Toronto, Ontario, Canada M4V 3B2
Penguin Books (N.Z.) Ltd, Cnr Rosedale and Airborne Roads,
Albany, Auckland 1310, New Zealand

Penguin Books Ltd, Registered Offices:
80 Strand, London WC2R 0RL, England

Published by Onyx, an imprint of New American Library,
a division of Penguin Group (USA) Inc. Previously published in a Dutton edition.

First Onyx Printing, April 2004
10 9 8 7 6 5 4 3 2 1

This is for Lisa, Jessica and Adam,
my lifeline to the real world.

1

Eddie knew he was invisible. He'd known it forever. He had seen himself disappear day after day, year after year.

They could all see him when he was young, back when he was a target. The ones who called him Fat Albert or Donkey Kong when he walked to the bus stop. The ones who would hold out their arms and puff up their cheeks and waddle. He'd hang his head, roll up his already thick shoulders and say nothing. He heard the words. He knew the grins in their faces, marked the golden chains around their necks, recognized all the logos, all the shoes.

They thought he was an idiot, too dumb to know who did what to who. Too stupid to know who was the owner and who was owned. But Eddie watched everything and everybody. He kept his head down, but his eyes were always cutting, this way and that. No one saw what he saw, every day and especially at night.

It was at night when Eddie first started to become invisible. Since he was twelve or thirteen he'd been roaming the night streets, and he'd always known every alley cut-through, every neighborhood fence, every streetlight shadow. Before long he knew without thinking about it; the timing on the traffic light at Twenty-fourth and Sunrise, when the last spray of summer sun came cutting through the empty lot of the rundown shopping center, when the streetlights flickered on and when the Blue Goose Beer Saloon closed and they brought out the last plastic barrel of garbage and leftovers.

In the dark Eddie knew where the dogs were kept and which ones he could feed raw meat scraps through the chain link and talk sweet and low to until they hummed and growled their own low throat noise back to him. Eddie's skin was darker than most of the others, and that's why he thought he could stand there, late at night in the shadows of a ficus tree or Bartrum's Junkyard fence, and stare into the bluish glow of someone's living room and never be noticed. When he was young, he did get caught. Old Man Jackson or Ms. Stone would come outside and yell from their porch, "Boy, get your self outta there and get on home. You ain't got no bidness out here now." And he would. Just walk away with no response. Just hunch up his shoulders and go.

When he quit school Eddie started hanging in the streets in the daytime. At fifteen he'd already grown into a big, thick man's body. He wore the same dark

T-shirt and dungarees nearly every day. His "workin' " clothes he called them. He walked everywhere he went. He never rode the bus. His mother never owned a car.

At some point he got hold of an abandoned shopping cart, sun flashing off chromed-up wire mesh, plastic handle name of Winn-Dixie. He would fill it with whatever pleased him: scrap metal and aluminum cans for profit, blankets and old coats for warmth, whiskey and wine bottles for company. He would push his cart through the alleys and streets and keep it next to him on the benches when he sat and everyone else got up and moved away.

Eddie would watch them all. People on their way to work. Mothers on their way to the clinic, kids in tow. Girls giggling and whispering secrets to each other. But soon, year after year, they stopped watching him. In time, Eddie became less than a neighborhood blemish. In time, he was a simple fact of life, a shuffling nothing.

Since they could not see him, Eddie had no fear of the night. That's why he now stood in the quiet dark of midnight under the royal poinciana that spread like a shroud over the corner bedroom of Ms. Philomena's house. He'd stood and watched as the lights had gone off one by one, until only the blue glow remained in the old woman's room. Still, Eddie waited. An hour. Two.

He knew Ms. Philomena. He had known her since he was a boy. She would walk her kids to the bus stop, dressed in her own workin' clothes; a long printed dress with a white apron and white shoes for her job on the east side. She was old even then. But Eddie never saw her out anymore. Only an occasional visitor, her daughter maybe, would stop to visit, and only in the day. Eddie would see Ms. Philomena's gray head just inside the door. He would watch her turn and slide her feet back and let them in. But now her daughter never knocked, she just unlocked and called out "Mama?" before disappearing inside. Eddie knew the old woman was weak. Tonight was her time.

He moved from his spot under the tree. No traffic had come down the alley for two hours. He crossed the narrow yard and knelt at the back jalousie windows of the Florida room and reached into his pockets for a pair of socks. He slipped them over each hand and then took a screwdriver from another pocket. Invisible in the shadows, he began the work of silently prying open the old, pitted aluminum clips that held each pane of glass in place. With the clips bent up, he could lift out each pane and carefully lay them in order on the ground outside. Eight panes out, and he was inside.

Eddie may have been a big man, but he was never clumsy. He had practiced all his life not to be clumsy. His movements were intentional and always precise. Once inside the house he stood breathing the odor of camphor and aged doilies, the scent of green tea and must from years of humidity and mold. The floors, like so many old Florida homes from the '60s, were hard, smooth terrazzo. No creaking wood. No popping joists. He moved down the hallway toward the glow. At the bedroom door he stopped to listen for breathing, something under the hiss of the television, a cough, a clearing of old phlegm. Nothing. Across the hall he could smell the scent of lilac soap drifting from the bath. He stood unmoving for several minutes until he was sure.

Inside, Ms. Philomena was laid out on the bed, her thin shoulders propped up on a corduroy-covered pillow. Her gray hair showed white in the TV light. Eddie could see her mouth hanging open in a slack O. The shadows on her caramel-colored skin made her eyes look sunken and her cheekbones sharp. She was nearly dead already, Eddie said to himself. He did not look at the old television screen. He knew it only robbed him of some night vision. He took careful steps to the bedside and with the socks still on both hands he laid his strong wide hands over Ms. Philomena's nose and mouth.

He was surprised how little she struggled, bucking her skinny chest only once, getting her fingertips barely into the material on his hands before that tiny whimper of death, when all went slack. Eddie didn't move. He just pressed his hands, only strong enough to keep the air cut off until he was sure. When he straightened, he placed Ms. Philomena's hand again atop her chest, adjusted her pillow and stepped away.

Outside again he carefully replaced the window-panes and, with his thumbs, bent back the clips. She was almost dead anyway, he whispered to himself. As he moved back to the alley, a breeze riffled through the canopy of the poinciana tree, shaking loose a shower of the famous flame-orange blossoms that had turned dark and wilted in the autumn coolness and now dropped like hot rain outside the old lady's bedroom window.

2

I was sitting, balanced in the stern seat of my canoe, letting twenty feet of fly-fishing line lay stripped out on the river. The vision of the silver sides of a tarpon was still behind my eyes, but I'd given up on trying to entice him out of the mangrove edges. Anyone who describes fly-fishing with adjectives such as grace and concentration and thoughtful skill without including dire patience is probably an equipment salesman.

An hour after I'd seen the bastard jump, I hadn't lured him into a single strike. I finally gave up, leaned back into the V of the canoe and let the morning South Florida sun melt into me. The odor of clean sweat mixed with the salt-tinged breeze and I took a slow, deep draw. I felt my heart rhythm tick down a beat and let it fall. I was shirtless and in a pair of canvas shorts. My legs long and tan except for the white knurled splotch of scar tissue on my thigh where a tumbling 9mm round had done a nasty work some time back. I closed my eyes to the memory, a place I didn't need to go. I might have dozed off but a subtle change in the sunlight, like a twist of a dimmer switch, caused a shiver in my skin. When I opened my eyes I was staring up at the western sky. An osprey was perched near the top of a dead sabal palm. The bird was staring back with a more focused intent. He may have been trying to figure out the floating fishing line, or, raptor that he is, trying to gauge the unmoving beast in the canoe. A wind shift caught both of our attentions and I turned to see an unusual October rainstorm rolling gray and flat out of the southeast. Summer storms came from the western Glades, sucking up fuel from the thin layer of water that covers thousands of acres of sawgrass. Anvil-shaped clouds then pushed to the coast as the cities and beaches warmed in the sun and the rising heat drew the cooler clouds east. But in the fall the pattern changed, storms came with more reason and threat, and something was swirling in the atmosphere.

A distant rumble of thunder caused me to sit up and start reeling in. Smart boaters and golfers know there is nowhere in the country with as many lightning strikes as Florida. I stowed the reel, picked up my hand-crafted maple paddle and spun the canoe west, heading toward the cavern-like opening in the mangroves and live oak that led into the canopied part of my river. The tarpon had waited me out. I'd have to test him another day.

On the open water I got into a rhythm—digging the paddle into the water, pulling the stroke full through and then feathering a clean kick at the end. Before I'd come here, the only paddling I'd ever done was when a fellow Philadelphia cop took me sculling on the Schuylkill River along boathouse row. It had been a fiasco until I got my balance and began to feel the water. Without my friend in the other seat of the double, I would have flipped a dozen times. But the quiet isolation on a liquid artery through the middle of the city was something I never forgot. Here, the canoe paddling was different, but the isolation had the same feeling.

I made it into the tree canopy just as the storm's first drops started pattering through the leaves. It was several degrees cooler in the shade tunnel, and I drifted while putting on an old Temple University T-shirt. It was also several shades darker on this part of the river, even more so with the sun slipping under storm clouds. This is an ancient river, running north through a flooded cypress forest before widening out through the mangroves and then flowing east out to sea. Inside it is a place of quiet water and the smells of wet wood and vegetation.

A mile in I slowed at a narrow water trail marked by two old-growth cypress trees. Fifty yards west, through shallow water and thick ferns, I pulled up to a platform dock attached to my stilt shack. I tied the canoe to a post and gathered my fishing gear. Before climbing the stairs I carefully checked the damp risers for footprints. I do not get company out here. No one else comes to my door.

Inside the single room it was dim, but I have so memorized its simple layout and content that I can find a matchbox with my eyes closed. I lit a single kerosene lantern and the glow grew just as fat raindrops started pinging off the tin roof.

When I first moved to this isolated place the rattling noise of showered tin had kept me awake for hours, but over the months the sound had turned somehow natural and sometimes I welcomed its heavy noise, if only to break the silence. At my potbellied wood stove I stirred some coals, started some kindling, and set a fresh pot of coffee to boil. While I waited, I stripped off my shirt and kicked out of my leather Docksides and sat at the wood-planked table. The air had gone thick and moist. I leaned back and propped my heels up on the table and surveyed: Bunk bed. Two warped armoires. A stainless-steel sink and drain board under a hanging row of mismatched cabinets. Old-style Key West shutters at the four windows on all sides and a high, pyramid-shaped ceiling topped with a slatted cupola to vent the rising warm air.

The shack had once been a hunting lodge for rich tourists in the early 1900s. It was passed to state researchers in the '50s, who used it as a home base for studying the surrounding ecosystem. It then lay abandoned for years, until my friend and attorney, Billy Manchester, somehow obtained the lease and rented it to me when I was searching for an escape from my Philadelphia past.

The only change I'd made was new screening and the installation of a wondrous trap Billy had found for the tiny gnats that could slip through the smallest barriers. One of his acquaintances, and Billy had hundreds, was a University of Florida researcher who'd cobbled together a CO_2 contraption to kill the no-see-ums. Knowing that it is the CO_2 that lures the insects to humans and other air-breathers, the researcher had configured a bucket-shaped container coated with a sticky oil and then inverted on a stem pedestal. Threaded with a CO_2 line, the stem emitted a small trail of gas, less than what two people talking would emit. The bugs came for the CO_2, got trapped in the oil, and I lived nearly unbitten on the edge of the Glades. I was ruminating on the simple genius of the idea when the rattle of my boiling coffeepot sat me up and then the electronic chirping of a cell phone made me curse. I went to the coffee first and then searched for the phone.

"Yeah?" I answered.

"Max," said Billy, his voice straight and efficient. "Max. I need your help."

3

In the morning I packed a gym bag with civilized clothes and a shaving kit and loaded my canoe. The sun was just beginning to streak through the high cypress cover, spackling the leaves and slowly igniting the greenness of the place. I untied and pushed off toward the river. The water was high from the rain. Dry ground was rare here, and the effect of the omnipresent water gave one a constant sense of floating. My shoulders and arms began to loosen after ten minutes of easy paddling. By the time I reached the open water I was ready to grind.

Billy had spent an hour on the phone explaining in his thorough and efficient way why he was making an uncharacteristic call for help. Billy is the most intelligent person I've ever met. A child chess prodigy from the north Philadelphia ghetto, he graduated top of his class at Temple's law school. He then took a second degree in business at Wharton.

He was an intellectually gifted black kid who grew

up in one of the most depressed and depressing areas of the country. I was an unambitious son of a cop who grew up in the ethnic, blue-color neighborhoods of South Philly. Our mothers had met and formed a quiet and unusual friendship, one that we had only begun to decipher as men. We did not meet until we made contact on new ground in South Florida, where, for our own reasons, both of us had fled.

I learned early to trust Billy. I also learned to listen carefully to his advice and his stories. He rarely said anything that wasn't thought out and worthy. I had kept that in mind last night as he spun through his reason for calling and I worked through the pot of coffee.

"You know it was Henry Flagler, Rockefeller's Standard Oil partner, who brought the first train down into South Florida?"

"No. But I do now," I said. "Go on."

"It was Flagler who pushed his tracks down the east coast to Palm Beach, where he built the largest winter resort in the world at the time for the rich and powerful New Yorkers like himself.

"Tough old guy," Billy said. "And pretty ballsy too."

There was reverence in his voice when he told how Flagler then took his rail line to Miami when it was just a fishing town, and then took on the superhuman task of building the overseas rail line from island to island all the way to Key West.

Some of this history I knew. Billy had been my lending library, passing on books about Florida's past, Audubon guides when I stared dumbly at a species I didn't know and maps to give me a larger idea of where I was. He rarely gave tutorials. But this felt different. My friend was a lawyer, he was building a case.

"Flagler employed thousands of southern blacks, free men who left their birth homes in Georgia and Alabama to hack his trail down the coast. They were the ones who piled the sand and gravel for a roadbed and then laid the ties and rails to carry Flagler's class to the sunshine."

"But better work than trying to scratch out the sand where they had been," I offered.

"Agreed," said Billy. "They weren't forced and they weren't stupid. But Flagler was also a businessman. He knew that deadheading empty trains back north wasn't profitable. So he encouraged and often subsidized farmers to grow citrus and winter vegetables on the land west of his tracks."

"So he could fill the empty trains going back north, and make a buck selling oranges in the winter," I said.

"Exactly. And once the rails were down, many of the black workers stayed and went to the fields to harvest that fruit and those winter vegetables."

For generations those families would be the muscled backbone for a thriving agricultural industry. It was not, we both knew, unlike the working core of North Philadelphia's factories and machine shops that once built thriving neighborhoods there.

"By the 1940s, stable communities were set west of Flagler's tracks," Billy went on. "And entrepreneurial women started small businesses, stores and restaurants that created an internal economy."

Billy's command of the facts was always solid, his

telling of the stories always eloquent, especially over the phone when he felt most comfortable. But deep into my fourth cup of coffee, I finally interrupted him.

"Wonderful history, Billy. And I appreciate your constant efforts to educate me. But your point is?"

He waited a few studied beats.

"The matriarchs, the ones who were forward-thinking and looked to guide and care for their family's future?" he said, hesitating, letting the leading question hang.

"Yes?"

"I think they are being killed."

I paddled for more than an hour, east and south toward the sea. The river water had turned a dull blue green and its banks changed from the low tangle of mangroves to sandy banks sprouting skinny pines. I was sweating heavily, but had perfected my strokes so that I could wipe the perspiration from my eyes with a swipe of my shoulder without breaking the rhythm. Since leaving the canopy the smell of brackish water had thickened and the east wind brought in the salt odor of the Atlantic. By the time I swung around the last bend and spotted the boat ramp at the ranger station, the morning sun was full, the dome of blue sky cloudless.

I sprinted the last 300 yards, digging deep and long, straining muscle and lungs until the blood pounded in my ears, and then I coasted into the graveled edge of land. I sat with my elbows on my knees and waited until my heart tripped down and my breathing eased

before I stepped out into ankle-deep water. I pulled the
boat up into a worn patch of shaded grass and pine
needles and unloaded.

The dock was empty but for the new ranger's
Boston Whaler tied up at one end. Further down the
river I could see a single fisherman in a bass boat
working the edges of an outcropping of pine root. I
shouldered my gym bag and walked up to the wash-
rooms and showered in hot water for the first time in
weeks. I shaved and then dressed in canvas pants, a
short-sleeved polo shirt and better Docksides. When I
came out I stopped just outside the doors and glanced
over to the ranger's office. No one appeared, even
though I knew the 24-hour shift man was on duty and
had seen me arrive. As I walked back to my canoe and
gathered the rest of my things, I could feel eyes on my
back. I crossed the parking lot and opened the cab
door to my midnight-blue pickup truck to let the heat
escape and tossed my bag in. I went back and flipped
the canoe under the shade tree, placed a black plastic
bag of trash I'd brought from the shack in a nearby
barrel and cut my eyes once to the windows of the
office.

Several months ago innocent blood had been spilled
on the river. An old and revered ranger and his young
assistant were killed. Some of it had been on my
hands. I believed it, and I could not blame others if
they shared that belief. I climbed into my truck and
pulled out of the parking lot, the white shell surface
crunching and popping under my tires.

*   *   *

Twenty minutes later I was climbing the entrance ramp to I-95 and, as always, dreading the traffic and the stench of exhaust in the urban world. Billy had asked me to meet him in his office just south of downtown. I dutifully stayed in my proper lanes, cruising south at the acceptable ten miles an hour over the speed limit, and slipped off the packed interstate onto an equally busy avenue. In downtown West Palm Beach I maneuvered through the one-way streets to a commercial block of high-rises that carried the names of banks and financial institutions on the façades. The buildings were all done in the same sandstone texture with the same contemporary block design. It was like a cookie-cutter Levittown gone vertical.

When I got to Billy's building I took the side entrance to the parking garage and stopped at the booth.

"Visitor's spots right there to the left," the attendant said after checking my name on a clipboard. He'd given me a pleasant enough smile in response when I'd given Billy's name, but like a trained street cop he'd also let his eyes roam my face and I could almost feel him reciting hair color, eyes, collared shirt and no tie. In my rearview I saw him taking down my tag number. It was a careful building.

I locked the truck and walked through a tiled passageway to the main lobby. There I ignored the scrutiny of the desk clerks and crossed to the bank of elevators, stepped in, and pushed 15. The entrance to Billy's suite was unmarked, just a double wood door of solid varnished oak. Inside the carpet was thick and simply patterned in a soft burgundy. There were several fine seventeenth-century English landscapes on the walls of the reception area that surrounded a large cherry wood desk. Behind a computer screen and a multi-button phone was Billy's secretary.

"Good morning, Mr. Freeman," she said, standing to reach over the desk to shake my hand. "A pleasure to see you again."

"It is always my pleasure, Allie."

"Thank you," she replied without a flutter. When Billy had first introduced me and told her where I lived and that I would have no mailing address, she'd seemed mildly amused. She was a third-generation Floridian, was creative and cultured and had only a cursory knowledge of the Everglades. The idea that a newcomer would live at its rough edge seemed a curiosity to her. The idea that the most dominating physical feature of an entire state could be ignored seemed to me an equal curiosity.

"Go right in, Mr. Freeman. He's waiting," she said. "I'll bring coffee."

Billy came around from behind his desk when I entered and smiled broadly. He was dressed impeccably in a starched, hand-tailored white shirt buttoned at the throat. His vest was brocaded in a swarm of subtle color. His suit pants were lightweight and charcoal, the matching coat was on a hanger. His shirt cuffs were rolled, carefully, twice.

"M-Max. Y-You are l-looking well," he said in his standard greeting.

It had taken me some time to get used to Billy's stutter, and only part of the effort had been because of the incongruity with his appearance and obvious success.

But the constant reminder was the way his speech pattern turned on and off. His is a tension stutter. On the phone, from the other side of a wall, even through a darkened doorway opening, his voice is clear, smooth and flawless. Face-to-face, his words clatter and fall from his mouth. The distinction seems a joke or a deception at first. But I learned early to listen to the words themselves, and judged him only by what he said, not how.

Billy was the one who'd convinced me to come to South Florida after bailing out of ten years and a family tradition with the Philadelphia Police Department. He was the one who invested my disability buyout into a profitable stock portfolio. He motioned to the leather sofa that faced the floor-to-ceiling windows looking out on the city.

I considered it a humbling debt to help Billy Manchester in any way I could.

"I h-h-hope m-my recitation last n-night was n-not too confusing," Billy said, bringing a stack of legal folders to the coffee table and sitting. "I have g-gathered as m-much information as there is, and it's n-not m-much."

He spread five folders out like a hand of cards. Fanning them with the tips of his fingers. I scanned through them. Each was labeled with a name. Some contained death certificates. Some included paramedics' run sheets and police reports. The medical examiner's reports were scant. The one similarity among them all was the cause of death: natural.

Allie came in with coffee and set the china service on

the table and then smiled when she slipped the large, flat-bottomed sailing mug in front of my place.

"I didn't forget how much you like your coffee, Mr. Freeman."

We both thanked her and Billy uncrossed his legs and poured. I thumbed through the documents again, hiding the growing skepticism I'd been pushing back all morning. All the women named in the case files were elderly. All over eighty. All lived in the same general area west of Fort Lauderdale. All were widows.

"Not much to go on here, Billy."

"I know. And that's w-what's wr-wrong. Not w-what's there, b-but w-what isn't."

He was up now, pacing as if in front of a jury, a place his brilliant lawyer's mind could make him a star but where his stutter had never let him go.

"An acquaintance came to m-me after the most recent death, her m-mother," he said. "At the funeral sh-she saw old f-friends. Longtime folks f-from the neighborhood. Her m-mother was somewhat p-prominent and it brought many of them together for the first t-time in years."

He was staring out the big windows. Outside the city spread out in the unbroken sunlight. Billy loved high views, and the thing about South Florida from a height was its complete lack of borders. No mountains or hills or even small rises, nothing but the horizon to hold it. Billy always looked out, he never succumbed to the natural urge to look down.

"The d-daughter c-came to me with questions about

the l-life insurance," he continued. "It had b-been sold. All of them had b-been sold."

I refilled my coffee, stacked the files again so each of the names lay exposed on top of one another. Billy had done some homework. The five women, all Florida born and raised, had lived somewhat similar lives, he said. They had grown up in the '30s and '40s, had raised families and worked well into their sixties. They had survived in a South Florida that in their time was a predominately Deep South society.

But all had also done an extraordinary thing. They had each bought life insurance policies for their families, sizable ones for their time, and had paid their premiums like clockwork. Then, late in life, they had inexplicably sold those long-held policies.

The viatical purchases were legal, Billy said. Each woman had been paid for the transfer to an investment company. Some had brought the women large windfalls. But the purchase price was only a part of the policy's worth. When the women finally died, the investors would cash in the policies for the full amount and walk away with the profit.

"All legal?" I asked, looking down at the names.

"P-Perfectly."

"And the twist?"

"The tw-twist is that the longer the insured lives, the more p-premiums the investors have to p-pay. That is w-why they usually look for medical infirmities, which all these w-women had," Billy said.

"But they m-might have underestimated the ttoughness of these ladies. The longer they lived, the more it cut into the investor's p-profit."

Billy was looking east now. In between the high rises, out past the Intracoastal Waterway to the red tile roofs of the beachfront mansions and estates of Palm Beach. I let him stand in silence, the dark skin of his profile a silhouette against the hot glass.

"You don't think that's kind of a shaky motive for murder?" I finally said.

He turned his dark eyes on me.

"M-Max. Since when has greed been a shaky m-motive?"

4

We walked up Atlantic Boulevard for lunch. The breeze had pulled the temperature down into the mid-seventies. An early lunch crowd was mixing on the street with women in business skirts, office workers in pressed white oxfords and cinched ties, and tourists in shorts and tropical prints floating from one window display to the next.

As we walked Billy explained how he'd tried to slip his theory in through the back door of the Broward Sheriff's Office. His contacts were extensive, but his pleadings fell on deaf ears. Drug enforcement, computer crime, demands from every sector to keep kids safe. School resource officers, traffic details in an overflowing maze of urban streets. Rapes, robberies and *real* homicides. Too much crime, too little time. "Bring me something with substance, Billy. Hell, the M.E. won't even go out on a limb." Even his political connections told him to back off. "It's not a good time to be screaming that they won't investigate crime in the black com-

munity. Not now, not with some *theory*, Billy. You got to
pick your battles." He'd hired a P.I. who after three
weeks came up with nothing: "I know that neighborhood, Billy, and nobody knows a damn thing about old
ladies getting killed."

The recitation of his dead ends pulled at Billy's face,
but still a knot of jaw muscle rippled in his cheek.
When I suggested his suspicions might best be handed
off to an insurance investigator, he was, as usual,
ahead of me. He had contacted several who worked
for the three different companies who insured the five
women. There had been little interest. They too had
written the deaths off as natural and paid out without
question. Only one of the companies, a small, independent firm, had agreed to send out a representative.
We were meeting him for lunch.

"I am s-sorry, M-Max. I'm asking too m-much. But I
only want your advice." Billy said. "You decide. I w-
will introduce you and b-be off."

Billy was not an ungracious man. I looked at him
when he said it. I know he felt my eyes on him.

"This is w-why I need your help," was his only
response.

As we approached Arturo's, one of Billy's favorite
sidewalk cafes, I could see a tall, thick-bodied man
pacing the curb in front. From a distance I thought of
one of those Russian nesting dolls, rounded at the
top and sloping down to a wide, heavy base. Ten
steps closer and I thought: lineman. His muscled
neck melted down from the ears into thick shoulders
and then, like a lava flow, down through the arms

and belly, settling in the buttocks and thighs. I had played some undistinguished football in high school at tight end. I knew from unsuccessful experience how hard it was to move such a man off that substantial base.

Ten more steps and I thought: ex-cop.

The man had turned our way, his head tilted down, one hand in his pocket, the other cupping a cigarette. He made himself look like someone lost in thought but I could see he was scanning the block, his eyes, in the shadow of his heavy brow, measuring every pedestrian, noting the makes of cars, marking those in parking spaces. Nothing entered his turf without being scrutinized. And that included us.

A few more steps and he took a final drag, flicked the cigarette into the gutter and squared to meet us.

"G-Good afternoon, Mr. McCane," Billy said, stopping short of handshaking distance. "This is M-Max Freeman, the gentleman I t-told you about."

McCane took my hand in a heavy, dry handshake.

"Frank McCane. Tidewater Insurance Company."

I nodded.

He had gray hair cut short to the scalp and looked to be in his mid-fifties. His face had a florid, jowly look. His nose had a broken bend as if from a quick meeting with a bottle. It also held a web of striated veins from a longer association with the same. But his facial features were overpowered by his eyes; pale gray to the point of being nearly colorless. They gave the impression of soaking in all the light that entered their field and reflecting back none. I am six-foot-three, and we were nearly eye to eye.

I held his gaze long after the appropriate time for a business handshake. Without a flinch of emotion his eyes moved off mine, focused on something behind my left shoulder, and then swung to the other side. Street cop, I thought. Street cops hate to be stared at. They need to know what's around them. I knew from walking a beat myself. Once a street cop, always a street cop.

As we stood on the sidewalk, Arturo approached from under the awning of his cafe. He had recognized Billy and knew how to treat an important customer.

"Ah. Mr. Manchester. Gentlemen, gentlemen. So good to see you, sirs," Arturo started, talking to us all but looking only at Billy. "May we seat your party please, Mr. Manchester?"

A gracious host, Arturo had taken Billy's hand in both of his and was guiding him toward a table.

"Arturo, gracias," Billy said. "P-Please take care of m-my guests. But I cannot s-stay."

"Of course, Mr. Manchester. I am disappointed but honored."

Billy turned to us.

"I have a m-meeting. Mr. McCane will fill you in, Max. I will sp-speak with you later."

I watched as Billy walked away. McCane had not moved from his spot on the sidewalk. When Arturo again extended his palm to an umbrella-shaded table, I turned to him.

"Let's eat."

The big man sat in a chair and then scraped the legs

across the flagstone so he could sit at an angle to the glass-topped table. He lit a cigarette and ordered "sweet tea." I asked the waiter for a Rolling Rock and McCane cut his eyes at me.

"Ya'll were on the job somewhere?" he said, the New York cop phrase sounding odd in his southern accent.

"Philadelphia. Ten years."

"Retired?"

"Quit," I said. "Took disability after a shooting."

"I seen that scar," he said, his eyes going to the penny-sized disc of scar tissue above my collarbone. I repressed the urge to touch the soft spot left by a bullet that had miraculously passed through my neck without killing me. I stared across the street, a flash of sun on the window of an opening door flickering behind my eye where the memory of the pale face of a dead twelve-year-old boy hid. I blinked away the vision.

"You?" I asked, turning back to McCane.

"Charleston P.D. for a while. Then over to Savannah some. Retired there. Picked up this investigative work through an old boy I knew for years. Money's all right. Don't like the travel much."

The waiter brought my beer with a glass. McCane sipped his tea, and refused to look as I took a deep draw from the bottle.

Out in the street a river of cars filled up the block and then flushed away with a change of the stoplight. It was a bustle, but unlike a fall day in a northeast city. The people weren't locked onto a destination; the subway, the train station, the office building where they could get out of the cold. Even on a busy downtown street here you can not stand under a blue sky next to a palm tree and be in too much of a hurry.

"Hard to find P.I. work down here?" he asked, taking another drag on his cigarette.

"I wouldn't know," I said, wondering how much Billy had told him about me. "Why do you ask?"

McCane released a lung-full of smoke.

"You know. Just figured if you had to work for him," he said, nodding in the direction Billy had walked, "things must be tight."

"It's a favor," I said, recognizing now the subtle edge of racism in the man's voice.

"Yeah, well," he said. "It all spends the same, don't it?"

The waiter came back for our orders. I asked for grilled yellowtail, knowing Arturo's chef would spice it nicely with a Cuban flavor.

"Black beans, sir?" the waiter asked.

"Yes, please."

McCane had not looked at the menu.

"I'll have the same," he said. "Nix the beans, heh?"

The waiter nodded politely and left. When he was gone McCane shifted into business mode.

The connection between two ex-cops was settled at arm's length. I now knew why Billy called me in to work with a man with whom he could not.

"My company owns three of the policies written on these women more than forty years," he started. "Some go-getter salesman comes down here in the '50s. Figures

Florida is boomin' what with all the young WWII vets makin' a new start.

"But he gets down here and the GIs and flyboys have already been scooped up by insurance companies with government connections. But this ol' boy ain't gonna waste a trip. He sniffs out another market and works the other side of the tracks, sellin' to the blacks who have a few bucks because the whole place is flush."

Again he seemed to stop a moment for effect.

"Got to give the boy some credit. He targeted the women. The housekeepers who had regular work in white homes. Shop owners who were runnin' little businesses. He sweet talks them with the old promise of security for the kids. Something for their future. A better life for them when you're gone. He signs up dozens of them, gets a few bucks up front, figures what the hell, they get a few premiums in before they quit paying, it's easy money."

I ate while McCane talked. I was listening, but watching other customers come and go, marking cars in traffic that held more than one male, and noting that each time I took a drink from my beer, McCane would look away. I was also thinking of Billy's history lesson.

"But some of these women kept up with their payments," I finally said.

"Yeah. And some even bought additional policies over the years. Especially this last one. Two hundred thousand worth when she sold to the viatical investors."

I finally cut to it: "You think someone killed them?"

"Hell, I don't know. The cops don't think so. The M.E. don't. But your boy Manchester does and he's got some kinda clout, cause here I am."

Billy's famous connections, I thought. But back in his office he'd admitted that without the cooperation and inside knowledge of the insurance carrier his abilities were limited. McCane picked at the fish, washing nearly every bite down with his tea.

"You know why Manchester's bringing you in on this? Cause unless you got some kinda inside track I don't know about, I'm not sure how it's gonna help," McCane said.

I didn't answer because I didn't know myself.

"Maybe you know people we can use for an inside look, cause I'm tellin' you, the incident reports are damn thin and I ain't gonna get shit from the relatives," McCane said. "To be honest, this is lookin' like a bad fishin' trip to me."

I drained my beer and came close to agreeing with him out loud. But I kept it to myself.

"I'll get with Billy," I said as the waiter cleared the table, presented the check and offered Cuban coffee as a parting gift from Arturo. I took the shot of sweet caffeine. McCane took the check and pulled out a silver clip of folded cash and refused my offer to split the cost.

"Expense money," he said with a slight grin. "They do take American, right?"

When I got back to Billy's office, he was still out. I left word with Allie that I'd call him as soon as I could and update him on my lunch with McCane. She raised her eyebrows at the mention of the insurance investigator's name.

"Will you be taking over for Mr. McCane?" she asked, an optimism in her voice.

The question caught me off guard. Billy knew how deep my vow had been to leave police work behind. He wouldn't have spoken openly about bringing me back in, even if that were his intention.

"I mean, it's just, you can see that he doesn't have much respect for Mr. Manchester," she said.

"He's Old South, Allie," I said. "Some people never leave it behind."

"I'm sorry. It's not my business," she said.

"No apology necessary."

As I turned to leave she said, "Have a nice day, Mr. Freeman."

I got my truck out of the garage, gave a short wave to the alert attendant, and headed back west. The heat of the day was rising off asphalt and concrete, parking lots and the tarred flat roofs of the myriad strip malls leading out through suburbia. The palms and sand pines did not lose their color in fall. The traffic would slowly increase with the number of winter migrants from the north. And like every place in America, the Christmas decorations would be up by Thanksgiving. My first winter holiday here I watched as a man pulled up next to me at a light with a Christmas tree from some tented lot stuffed in the open back seat of his convertible. I knew he was smiling because it was 30 degrees and snowing back in New York. But it still didn't seem right.

I kicked the A.C. up and the outside temperature on my dash readout said 79. Farther west I pulled into a plaza grocery and loaded up with supplies: coffee and canned fruit, a few vegetables and thick loaves of dark bread. Sometimes I stayed out at the shack for a month at a time without coming in. But I had the feeling I'd be back to the city soon enough. When Billy got onto something, he was relentless. If he wanted me in on this, whether to prove or disprove his suspicion, he'd have a plan.

By the time I reached the boat ramp the sun was on its downward slide. A ragged ceiling of high cloud was drifting over the Glades, its edges already glowing with streaks of pink and purple. I flipped my canoe and started loading. I was lacing a small waterproof tarp over the groceries in the bow when I heard the crunch of footsteps on the shell growing louder behind me.

"Mr. Freeman?"

I turned to face the new ranger, a man in his thirties with thick blonde hair and creases at the corners of his eyes from hours of squinting into hard sunlight. He was about six feet tall, lean and tanned and dressed in uniform. His hand came up with an envelope as he stepped up and stopped.

"The Park Service wants a copy of this to go to you, sir."

"And what might this be?" I asked, taking the white business-sized letter, but not looking down from the ranger's eyes.

"You'll have to read it, sir. A copy has also gone to your attorney. My understanding is that the state is attempting to break your lease on the research station, sir."

"And why would the state be interested in doing that, Mr., uh, Griggs?" I said, reading from the nameplate mounted above the ranger's pocket.

"I don't know, sir," he replied. "I was only asked to deliver the mail, sir."

Still I did not move my eyes off his. Everyone knew of the incident surrounding the death of the former ranger and his apprentice. They were killed with my gun. The shooter, who had been dubbed "the midnight murderer" by the press, had been after me and had later been stabbed to death on the river. The violence put a stain on this pristine place that I could not deny.

I held the new ranger's gaze for a moment longer before folding the letter and stuffing it into my back pocket.

"Thanks," I said.

Griggs turned without a response and walked unhurried back to his office. I locked my truck, scraped the canoe down the ramp and pushed off onto the dark water. Twenty minutes out I stopped stroking and drifted, my paddle dripping a trail of water on the flat surface like beads slipping off a string.

The air was damp and still. I had stopped just at the point in the river where the tidal change pushed and pulled at the fresh water flowing from the Glades. The smell was unique, like moist, fresh-turned soil, and I breathed deep and closed my eyes, trying to wash away the feel of the city. But the mental grinding that was my constant companion was back at work. I couldn't pull an image of Billy's dead women into my head. I'd seen too many bodies in my ten years as a cop on the Philadelphia streets: gunshot wounds and beating victims, suicide jumpers and elderly people who simply died from heat stroke in their choking tenement buildings. I'd had enough. But if he was right, could I turn him down?

Billy had a way of picking up all the linear facts while the emotional parts sometimes slipped by him. Maybe I could just talk with Billy's client, the one who'd lost her mother. Hear her out, get my own feel before dismissing my friend's theory. McCane sure as hell wasn't going to gain anything from the relatives. People with a past in it can smell racism on a man. He would get no further than the fake politician, the shop foreman or the field boss. The stink was on him in ways he probably didn't know. I might not be anymore successful talking with the grieving daughter, but I was sure I couldn't do worse.

I shifted in the canoe, the movement sending out a ripple off the gunwales as I reached into my back pocket for the envelope. Tearing it open made an odd and unnatural sound out here, and a Florida red-belly turtle reacted, sliding off his spot on a downed tree trunk into the water.

I unfolded a legal notice of a filing by the State of Florida against the lessee of property lot #6132907 in sec. 411. The petitioner was filing to break the ninety-nine-year lease of said property and all special conditions set within, claiming an intrusion on said property contained within the boundary of a designated state park and possible deterrents of such included property and riparian areas contiguous to said property.

The suit was copied to Billy. He'd know the legalese. But I could translate well enough. They were trying to kick me off my river.

5

That night I dreamed of sleeping in the old brass bed with a down comforter pulled up against the cold. The baseboard heater was ticking as its metal expanded and then contracted in its nightlong work against leaky windows and weather stripping. But the shrill ringing was a different, jarring sound. I fumbled with the phone and muttered into the receiver and my father's graveled, booze-laced voice was on the other end.

"Get the fuck up, patrolman. There's an officer down three blocks from your damned town house at Camac and Locust."

In my dream I am up on the side of the bed pulling on a pair of jeans, my father's command like a whip crack that has snapped me into motion since early childhood. I yank my boots over bare feet and clomp down the narrow staircase, pulling on a sweatshirt and banging a knee on the wrought-iron railing at the bottom. What the hell is he talking about? Camac and Locust. Christ, what time is it? Officer down?

I fumble with my keys, unlock the bottom kitchen drawer and pull my holster and 9mm out and strap the leather on. I grab my police department jacket off the hook and when I open the back door to the court-yard the winter air stings my face and I am running and still shaking the sleep out of my head when I hit the curb on Alder.

It's dark and I can tell by the empty street that it is well after 2:00 A.M. Doc Watson's on Eleventh is closed. Bar stragglers are gone. The street lamps on the corners near the Jefferson Hospital Library are glowing a soft orange and the block is silent but for the one urgent yelp of a siren growing louder in the distance.

I manage the corner of Locust and look to the west toward Broad and four blocks down is a patrol car, light bar spinning, sitting across the one-way street, its headlights painting two bright globes on the wall of the one-hour dry cleaning place. I start running along the edge of the parked cars when the ambulance from Jefferson comes wailing around the corner and the second, no, third, patrol car screeches up on the scene and I see two officers jump out with weapons drawn and I reflexively reach down for my own.

Another block closer and I see the other patrol car, dark against the corner, a knot of guys on their knees at the trunk, their hands busy with something on the ground, their faces bobbing up into the light, their voices sounding too anxious for cops. One gets up and starts directing the ambulance and his wet hands are glistening in the headlights and now I'm thirty feet away.

"Christ, hurry up, man, hurry," one is snapping. "Get the goddamn stretcher."

"Keep pressure on the chest, pressure," says another.

"You're cool, Danny. You're cool, man. We got you, man. You're cool," says another.

The paramedics are out with their bags. When I get twenty feet away the backup cops standing at the other side of the group pick up my movement and their guns come up and I am in three sight-irons.

"Cop. I'm a cop," I yell, palms going up and wide so they can see my empty hands and my jacket. The other officers and paramedics look up only for a second and then are back to their focus. On the ground behind his squad car I see Danny Riley. He's on his back, his eyes shut, skin gone white in the lamplight. Another officer has ripped open his jacket and is pushing a reddening towel into his chest and the medics are trying to take vitals and one is saying, "Fuck it. Let's get him to Jeff. We're only four blocks away—let's go."

And now all of us but the two backup officers are lifting Riley onto the stretcher and he feels so light with all the hands working that I think to myself, He's too light, he must be dead.

In seconds we have him in and the ambulance pulls away and we're all just staring after it when two more units come swinging in from the north and south. In the crosshatching headlights the intersection is glowing and I am looking around for a familiar face when the mood and attention of the gathering shifts.

For the first time I see what the backup guys are focused on. Their guns are still loosely pointed at a black man sitting on the curb. His legs are stretched out into the street. His head is bent to his chest and long ropes of braided hair are dangling into his lap. His hands are cuffed behind him and one shoulder is oddly twisted. The material of his coat sleeve is soaked and dark. Eight feet away a chrome-plated handgun lies on the sidewalk.

The uniformed guys are standing back. Not one of us from the group that lifted Riley takes a step closer. I turn to the cop holding the blood-soaked towel and ask what the hell happened.

"Fuckin' homeboy shot Danny Riley in a traffic stop's what happened. Danny got a round off and wounded him but the motherfucker put a kill shot into Danny while he was down."

The newly arrived cops are getting the same story. I watch their faces change from an intent listening to an anger that tightens their jaw muscles and narrows their eyes, and when they cut their looks at the wounded man on the curb I know I am looking at my own face in an angry mirror.

A second ambulance pulls up. A police step van right behind it. A sergeant has appeared from somewhere and some of us gather around him as the cop with the towel fills him in. The paramedics climb out of the second unit and approach, watching us, watching the wounded suspect, watching the guns still unholstered.

"Got a guy needs attention here, Sarge," the first medic says, and it is not a question. The sergeant raises one finger to silence him.

"We're securing the scene, doc," he says.

We all watch as the sergeant looks around at the high windows of the darkened buildings around us. He walks slowly over to the sidewalk, scans the area and then walks back to his squad car. He is the ranking officer on the scene. Everyone else is silent as we watch him reach into his car and come out with a plastic evidence bag. He is in no hurry, and even the paramedics seem to be unable to speak. We all watch him walk back toward the suspect and past him to the chrome handgun. He stares at it a full minute and then bends to pick it up and place it carefully in the bag.

He stands and seals it.

"OK. Secure," he says, pointing at the group of officers, "Put him in the van."

All four of us walk over to the black man and grab a piece. I'm left with the bloodied shoulder but I don't care. When we pull him off the curb a low keening of pain rises in his throat and he is heavy and nearly limp. Someone grabs his belt and we drag him across the street to the open van doors and the keening becomes a wail. A cop up inside reaches out and takes a fistful of dreadlocks and yanks as we all boost him into the truck and someone gives him a final shove with a boot to his haunch. The doors slam shut and when I bang my palm on the side panel I turn and see that both the paramedics and the sergeant have turned their backs to the scene. The van pulls away in the direction of the hospital. Towel man catches my eye and then tracks down my arm. I look down to see the blood smear on my hand from the black man's wound and the cop carefully folds the towel with Danny Riley's blood and walks away.

When I wake up the shack is still and the cool night air has drifted in and pushed out the heat but I am still sweating and I know there will be no more sleep this night.

I pull on a pair of jeans. In the swamp outside it's the dead-zone time, a strange biological warp that shrouds this place long after midnight but far from dawn. It's a time when the insects stop their chirping. The night predators have given up. And the early hunters and daytime foragers are still asleep. The quiet is like a pressure on the ears. I interrupt it with the hiss of propane and light the portable stove to heat my coffee.

That night in Philadelphia, Danny Riley would die and the shooter would find ignominious celebrity in the years to follow. He would claim innocence and racism. The courts would end up on trial. The wounded man, the one who knew the truth, would never speak it.

I poured a cup of coffee and stepped out onto the landing to sip it. I stared into the canopy and remembered the scene in the emergency room waiting area that had filled with cops and wives and reporters and camera crews. When the police chief came out surrounded by his captains he made a terse and tearful statement, announcing that Riley had succumbed to his wounds. There was an almost group exhalation, a beat of mutual pain that was interrupted by the blonde radio news reporter who asked the first question:

"Chief, what do you say to the reports that your officers took an inordinate amount of time to transport the wounded suspect and that they beat him before tossing him bodily into the paddy wagon?"

Everyone in earshot turned to look at her and when I did I saw my father, out of uniform, standing near the wall with two of his precinct friends. He was staring at me, nodding his head and smirking with an unfamiliar "atta boy" that he rarely had cause to waste on me.

I'd gone through the coffee by the time the morning was old enough to call Billy. I had tried him several times during the evening but knew that by seven he would be up and sitting on the oceanfront patio of his high-rise apartment going through the *Wall Street Journal*.

"Counselor."

"Max. Just taking a look at some of these tech stocks that I got you out of two years ago. It may be an opportune time to sneak back in on some of the safe ones to keep things moving in your portfolio. No more of this holding your own and getting savings account level returns. Even we conservatives have to get in the water again."

"Who ever called you a conservative, Billy?"

"Only those who can't figure out how I stay ahead, my friend."

"OK. Then let's move ahead, Mr. Greenspan. What's your plan with this McCane guy, and what do you want me to do that you or he haven't already done?"

I watched an early heron slide its snake-like neck into a patch of water hyacinth while Billy shifted gears. "I don't know how serious McCane and his company are. Maybe no more than the police or the prosecutor's office. Maybe he's just here on the company dime, soaking up the sun and pretending to be working."

"I don't see a whole lot of enthusiasm," I said. Billy hesitated.

"You know I don't ask you into this easily, Max. I thought I could get to it, track it down from the outside."

He listened to my silence.

"My feeling is the answers are in the street, and I admit I won't go there anymore, Max. It doesn't work for me."

My friend had made his escape. I wondered if he knew something I didn't, if he knew I couldn't make mine. Maybe he was right.

I told him I wanted to start in the neighborhood, with the daughter who had first called him in.

"Logical," he said, his voice losing its tension. "McCane has already been over there and wasn't too subtle."

I could imagine the stone-cold looks and the long-ago images of "the man" that would run through most of the minds in such a place when McCane came banging on the door.

"No doubt," I said. "I'm sure that loosened things up nicely for me."

"I'll talk to Ms. Jackson's daughter about you."

When I let the statement sit quiet for a few seconds, he added, "Thanks, Max."

"You are my attorney," I said. "And by the way, as such, what the hell is going on with this petition to kick me out of my place?"

I could hear him on the other end, could picture him taking a long draw on one of those fruit and vitamin drinks he had every morning. "How hard do you want me to fight it?" he asked.

Billy thought my isolation on the river was therapeutic when I first came south. The ghost with a dead boy's face, my bullet in his chest, was lodged hard in my head. The river was a cloak against it. Every night I had tried to grind the vision out with late night paddlings up and down the river that were almost manic with effort. But the sweat and pounding of blood in my ears had not saved me. Obviously my friend thought it was time for me to come out and rejoin the world. I wasn't sure I wanted to.

"Fight it," I finally said. "I still need some time to work on my casting technique."

6

By 10:00 A.M. I was back in my truck, sitting at a four-way stop in an old, unincorporated section of Broward County, Ms. Jackson's address in my hand. The streets were numbered in progression to the west. The neighborhood was several blocks north of Sistrunk Boulevard, which was considered the main commercial strip in the community. It was here that the black merchants built thriving businesses at a time when separation was still a way of life in the Old South. The street had eventually been named after Dr. James Franklin Sistrunk, one of the first African-American doctors in the county, who practiced when blacks were still banned from being treated in white hospitals on the east side.

I eased the truck onto Northwest Seventeenth Avenue and started looking for numbers. The asphalt street was a dull gray in the high morning sun. There were no sidewalks, and the graveled swale that ran along both sides was a dusty white in the glare. Small, single-story block houses sat back off the roadway. The front lawns were dry and bare. There was a distinct lack of trees on the front lots, but I could see a line of spreading ficus and an occasional poinciana swelling up above the shingled roofs in the back.

There was one such tree on the corner of the next block, and three men were gathered in its shade.

The two standing were young, in their late teens, and their heads turned my way as I rolled up and then snapped the opposite way as if my arrival might automatically bring a squad car from the other direction. The third was sitting in a metal folding chair, his legs splayed out, one hand dangling down, the other folded in the vicinity of his crotch.

He faced the street, and although there were three or four other bent and rusted chairs empty around him, the other two remained standing, their hands in their pockets, their backs turned to the street and to me. As I passed, the sitting man checked me out using the torsos of his boys as bad cover for his surveillance. It was a scene being played out on thousands of corners all over the country, I thought. At Third and Indiana in Philly, at the Triangle in Miami. But unlike the open markets of the 1980s, when the sellers would put their faces in any car window that rolled down the street, the new breed were far more careful. They didn't sell to strangers, at least not on the first pass.

I drifted through the intersection and in the rearview all three had turned to watch me. Farther down the block I spotted the set of numbers I was searching for and pulled into the driveway behind a new four-door sedan, deep green and freshly waxed. My knock on the door brought a response from deep in the house.

"Just a second, baby."

The small porch was barely covered by the overhang. A pair of women's shoes was lined carefully on a rough mat. There was a white plastic chair and matching cocktail table with a cheap Japanese fan folded and resting on the yellowed top.

The woman was halfway into another sentence when she opened the door and looked up into my face, stared for a fleeting second, and then blushed.

"Oh. Excuse me. I was . . . Well, you must be Mr. Freeman. Correct?"

"Yes, ma'am. Max Freeman," I said, offering my hand.

"Please come in Mr. Freeman. I'm Mary Greenwood. Mr. Manchester told me you would be coming by," she said, losing the flush quickly and becoming formal.

She was a stout woman. The light brown skin of her face was smooth and unblemished. She could have been thirty or fifty. She led the way through a darkened living room crowded with heavy upholstered chairs, an ancient standup piano and lamps with tasseled shades. The walls were crowded with shelves of photos and ceramic knickknacks with religious themes. An oil painting of Jesus dominated one wall. A portrait of Martin Luther King, Jr., another.

"This was my momma's house," she said, moving into the small kitchen. "Shared it with my father for his last years and refused to move out after he passed."

She moved to the counter and started working at an old ceramic coffeepot, white with a blue cornflower pattern.

"Coffee?" she said, taking the lid off the stemmed metal basket and spooning a dark blend out of a glass container.

"Thank you," I said. "The paperwork Mr. Manchester had said your mother was eighty-four?"

"That's right."

"And she passed away sleeping in her bed, what, eight years after her husband's death?"

She was silent. She'd heard the rationalizations from the medical examiner, the prosecutor's office, the police investigators. Too many times from too many officials.

"Since you said yes to the coffee, Mr. Freeman, let's us go on out back and I will tell you about my momma and why I do not believe the Lord called her this way."

"A pleasure, ma'am," I said.

She brought the coffee out onto a back porch, a slab of concrete set up with the same plastic furniture as the front. The backyard was shaded by the row of trees. A ragged ficus hedge gave the lawn a small privacy. The fanned-out poinciana, its leaf pattern as intricate as a doily, spread out over half the yard, and blooming jasmine spotted the deepest corner with yellow globs of color.

Philomena Jackson's daughter settled into one of the chairs, looked out onto the yard, took a deep breath of the garden air, and began.

"My momma was a prideful woman, Mr. Freeman.

She moved to Florida with her family when she was just a little girl. Her father, my grandfather, was a strong, intelligent truck farmer from Georgia. He could read and write and was good at organizing men of his own color and had little trouble finding work in the bean fields of west Pompano Beach.

"He could roll through the rows of vegetables in the heat of the day like a big ol' iron machine, momma said. He could pick and stack as much as three men and smile and hum his way through the gospel dawn to dusk. His family joined him. My mother was in the fields at age seven. Right next to her own momma.

"It wasn't long before my grandfather's organizing talents were recognized, and in the early 1920s he was made a foreman. He knew how to drive a flatbed truck and, starting with his own family, would pick up a dozen or more folks along old Hammondville Road and get them to the fields by sunlight. At the end of the day he would assist with the counting and ledger-keeping so my momma and grandmother would walk back home on the dirt track all the way back to their house and get to making dinner. They made fifteen cents a bushel picking."

She paused to refill my cup. I was still considered a newcomer to South Florida, but under Billy's pushy tutelage, I'd become a fan of the area's short, barely one-hundred-year history. Ms. Greenwood told the stories with a flawless memory forged of repetition, bed-time recreations and dinner table discussions. I could not see McCane sitting here, with a middle-aged black woman, listening with any form of discerning ear.

"One day, when Momma was only nine, she and my grandmother went to a store near the railroad track to shop. They'd gone there for years but this day a new owner had taken over. When they got to the front door the man looked up from his counter and said, 'Ya'll go round back and they'll take care of you.'

"Momma said grandmother just stopped and stared, not uttering a word. The man looked up again. 'They's new management now. Ya'll coloreds got to go round back.'

"Momma said she could feel grandma's hand tighten around her own, but nothing came from her lips and finally it was my momma who turned her eyes to the man and said 'No, sir.' And they both turned and walked, hand in hand, back to their house.

"When they told my grandfather, who was by now a respected foreman, he said he'd take care of it. But the women had something else in their heads. In a month they'd set themselves up a wooden building right along the dirt road that led to the fields and stocked it with flour and coontie and molasses and bags of processed cane sugar. Their store was one of the first black-owned businesses in the area and no one, black or white, ever went around to the back door."

She looked out in silence into the greenness of her late mother's yard, then spoke to whatever vision she was seeing there.

"My momma was not a weak woman, Mr. Freeman. She did not hold much to depending on others. I suppose I should have been strong enough myself to make her come live with me instead of letting her stay in this old house, but she was hardheaded. Too hardheaded for me."

I shifted my chair, using the scraping sound to bring her back.

"Did she ever mention this life insurance deal to you? Explain why or how she came to sell it?"

A wry grin came to the corner of her mouth and she slowly shook her head.

"I'd like to say I should have known, but I didn't have any idea such a thing could be done. About three years ago, I must have been whinin', tellin' Momma about trying to get the money together for my son's freshman year at the university. I was probably grumbling about wages at the hospital, cryin' about the mileage on the car. She took it in, like she always did. When we were kids, she'd tell us to shut up and be thankful for the things we did have. But you know, somehow, a little something extra would show up for a birthday or at Christmastime. That was her way. So then about two years ago, out of nowhere, comes a bank note. A present, she says, for her grandson's tuition, $20,000 to get him through four years. She hands it to my son and then to me she gives a $18,000 cashier's check and says 'Here's your car, baby. You got to pick it out.'

"Now, we always knew Momma hoarded and saved money. She was the one who somehow paid my first year to nursing school. This time she told us it was money from insurance, but she said it was from a policy on my father, and that she'd kept it since he died.

She wanted to give it to us. She felt it was an important time in our lives to have it and it was important to her that we did have it."

She stopped and looked me in the eyes. Her own were tight and dry.

"Only half of her explanation was the truth, Mr. Freeman. But when she got her mind made up, you didn't argue with Momma."

"And you didn't find out about her selling her own policy until after her death?" I said.

"We had Mr. Manchester go through her things. He found it."

"But you were already suspicious?"

My question forced her lips into a hard sealed line and I could see the muscle in her jaw flex.

"My mother was not in good health, Mr. Freeman. She had cancer and she knew it was coming. But she was not ready to die. When I walked into this house it did not smell of death, it smelled of violation," she said. "When I found her on her bed I could not feel peace. I could, in my bones, feel anguish. I don't care what the medical examiner says. I will go to my own grave believing my mother was killed."

All I could do was nod.

"Yes, ma'am. I can appreciate that."

She did not offer more coffee and I was relieved not to have to decline. We both pushed back our chairs and she led me around outside, past the old-time Florida room, to the front of the house.

"I hope I have been of some help, Mr. Freeman."

"Yes, ma'am, you have," I said.

We cleared the front corner and I saw them over her shoulder, the three men from the corner. They were in the street at the end of the driveway, hands in their pockets, heads bent together like they were in some loose football huddle.

When she spotted them Ms. Greenwood raised her voice.

"Beans, what you want?"

The middle one, the leader, stepped out.

"What up, Ms. Mary?" he said, his eyes acknowledging her and cutting to me to define his question.

"This is Mr. Freeman. He's a friend of Ms. Philomena. He's helping me."

All three of them took me in, head to toe, as if they could judge the truth of her statement by the cut of my clothes.

"Alright, Ms. Mary. You say so," the leader said and led his troop back toward the corner.

I turned back to her as I unlocked my truck.

"Neighborhood security?" I said, motioning to their backs.

A grin, part amused and part deprecating, pulled at the corners of her mouth.

"Respect," she said.

Again, any response would only show my own ignorance. I climbed in the truck and backed away.

7

Eddie was leaving the west side dope hole, his business with the Brown Man done.

Eddie knew all the dealers near his neighborhood, had done business with them, and those who proceeded them, and those who proceeded them. When he was a kid he was a huffer, getting high on glue shoplifted from one of those craft stores and then squirted into a plastic sandwich bag. Breathing in the fumes he could make it through the days just floating, not ever hungry, always moving, never in one place, just drifting through the streets, becoming invisible.

He'd picked up the huffing habit by watching. Kids behind the ficus hedges at the bus stop, older dropouts in the alley behind Murcheson's Gas Station. He watched, his face down and eyes probing. When they left he'd inspect their trash, figure out their methods and find out a way to get his own, because Eddie was not stupid. Eddie could always find a way.

When he got older he moved up to smoking weed,

drinking whatever booze he could steal from his mother's house or find discarded in the backstreet bins. The day he watched a young white couple being taught by one of the neighborhood dealers to smoke cocaine from a tiny metal pipe was a turning point Eddie never saw coming.

Crack.

The first time was a wonder to him. The high soaked into his head and body like a huff of glue gone wild. It burned his insides with a tingle and a rush that rolled him back on the milk crate he was sitting on and turned the whole alley into a soft place racing with a warm fire. And when it passed, Eddie wanted more, and more.

He would get ripped off in the early days. He'd scrape together the money, steal when he could, run his routes through the northwest neighborhoods picking up aluminum and metal to recycle for a few bucks, and then head for the dope man. The early ones would overcharge him, or give him bad shit. They'd give him chunks of soap and even ground bones to pass for crack. But Eddie learned from his mistakes. His mother had taught him early not to let anyone take advantage of him, and unlike so many junkies, the drugs did not diminish Eddie. By the time he was seventeen he was thick and strong and the deep tunnel of his stare caused most of the dealers to simply give him his due and get his unsettling presence off their corners.

But the crack finally scared him. Eddie did not like the way it blinded him. He would find himself in places he didn't know, trying to recognize people he should have known. The randomness of it unsettled and scared him. Eddie liked routine, it was how he survived. His discovery of heroin was his savior. A drug he could use and still move through the night streets, feeling painless, carrying out his work, keeping his eyes tuned. His routine was his cloak and his slow dark visage did not carry a reputation off the streets. He remained quiet, silently invisible to most of the world.

Today the Brown Man had been equally silent when Eddie came for his heroin. The dealer had seen him two blocks away, pushing his shopping cart along the edge of the street, one defective wheel clattering and spinning wildly each time it lost purchase with the concrete. The Brown Man swept the area with a knowing eye for any hiccup in the routine and then, satisfied, elbowed his new runner.

"Bundle," he said, and the boy looked expectantly down the street and then wrinkled his face at the lack of traffic.

"Go on, nigger," snapped the dealer, cuffing the boy with the back of his hand and scowling after him until he'd disappeared around the fence. As Eddie rattled closer, the dealer reached into his pocket and took out a gold dollar coin and started flipping and rolling it in his hand. He had worked the street for two years, dealt with the meanest motherfuckers in the biz. Been tightened up by the cops a dozen times and just swallowed the blood in his mouth and stayed cool. But the trash man always made him nervous. Those got-damn eyes lookin' up at you like dark holes that you couldn't escape.

The boy came back just as Eddie slowed to a stop, his cart inches from the Brown Man's hip. The runner started to offer up a warning to the old junk man but the dealer hushed him. The Brown Man took the thirteen dime bags of heroin from the boy and dropped them casually into the cart. In exchange Eddie passed him a crisp, folded hundred-dollar bill. Neither man spoke a word. Eddie shuffled on and the boy's eyes rode his rounded back until he was out of earshot.

"They's a man you don't fuck with," the Brown Man said when the runner turned. "His money's always good, and you don't never try to cheat his ass. You always give him the good rate, hear?"

The boy nodded. He was new, only on the street a week, but he had never seen such deference from the Brown Man, even when the packed-up low riders or the sedans with white men pulled up. Maybe it was the junk man's eyes, the boy thought. He'd never seen eyes so hollow.

Five blocks later Eddie heard the girl behind him. He'd seen her peeking out of the alley when he went by. He knew she would follow. Now she was hanging back, scared but unable to stop herself. Eddie went left, around the chain link fence at the back property of the old newspaper printing plant and pushed his cart a few blocks through the alley. He turned onto a rutted trail leading into an overgrown weed lot. There was an abandoned cinder-block shack squatted down near the back of the lot. It had once been some kind of electrical substation, but once it had gone unused for a month, it was stripped of anything that could be used, exchanged or sold. Eddie hoped no crackheads were using it. He could hear the girl moving in the grass behind him. He pushed the cart against the outside wall of the blockhouse and ducked through the doorway.

Inside the single room a torn, filthy mattress lay on the floor. Piles of wadded trash—greasy food wrappers and empty cellophane bags—were kicked into the corners. Something scurried away when Eddie sat down on one corner of the mattress and took out his tools.

Inside his coat was a spoon from his mother's kitchen, a small bottle of water and a syringe that he had stolen from her diabetic supplies. Eddie knew the value of a clean needle. Sometimes he could barter the ones he had hoarded in exchange for dope when times were tough. But times had not been tough. Eddie had money now. He carefully poured the water into his spoon and then mixed in the powder from one of the thirteen bags. He wondered what was taking the girl so long.

When the heroin was ready, he took out a small piece of cotton from his shirt pocket and rolled it between his thumb and finger into a small ball. He dropped the cotton into the spoon and set it on the floor while he took the orange cap off the syringe and then she was there.

"Hey baby, you got some sugar for me, too?"

The girl was leaning into the doorway, the toe of one shoe pointed carefully inside. She had finger-brushed her hair back and used some kind of cloth to wipe her face clean. When Eddie looked up she straightened her back, pushing her small breasts out against the worn fabric of a dingy cotton blouse. Eddie could see the tremble in her fingers.

"I seen you stop off at the Brown Man's so I was wonderin' maybe you want some company," she said, trying to hold her voice steady. Eddie went back to his spoon and slipped the needle into the soaked cotton and drew the liquid up into the syringe. The girl stepped over and sat next to him, folding her long, washed-out skirt under her. From somewhere she came up with a thick rubber band and without asking wrapped it around her bare upper arm. Eddie looked into her face but she was staring at the needle, a small pink tip of her tongue showing at the corner of her mouth.

"You get what you want. I gets what I want," Eddie said.

Question or order? The girl couldn't distinguish the statement. But she knew how to handle his kind. She'd been on the street. She'd get the sweet shot and slip the junk man without giving anything up.

"Sure, baby. I know what you want, big man," she said without looking up from the needle. The veins in her arm had popped like thin worms under her bruised skin. She nodded and the tip of her tongue moved to the other corner.

Eddie watched the girl accept the dose of heroin into a thin vein. He watched her eyes roll up and the smile play at her face. He liked to watch them. It made him anxious for his own hit, but he liked to see them smile first. She hummed through the high for a few minutes and then her eyes drifted open.

"Go 'head, baby," she slurred. "Get your own self some of this."

Eddie knew the girl would wait until he was half conscious with a dose and then either rip him off or split. He shook his head.

"Now I gets what I want."

The girl's eyes opened wider and she pulled herself up.

"Okay, baby. You gonna get yours. But I gotta pee first. Know what I mean?" She was now on her feet. Yeah, Eddie thought, I know what you mean.

She took a step and he had her by the wrist before she could turn. She kicked at him but Eddie caught her ankle and like a rag doll tossed her back on the mattress. Eddie had been cheated too many times by women. When she started to scream Eddie had her instantly by the throat. No yellin'. Ain't no yellin' in this house, his mamma always said. His grip on her throat tightened until she was quiet and he went about his business, getting what was his.

When he was through, Eddie let loose and sat back against the cool block wall. The girl stayed quiet while he mixed his own package from the bundle and got himself high. She was still quiet when he got up to leave. She was still lying there when he ducked out the doorway and started pushing his cart back to the streets.

8

When I left Ms. Greenwood I drove east, over the tracks and toward the ocean. After ten years as a cop I'd heard enough stories, confessions, excuses and bullshit to come to a conclusion. Truth is an ephemeral thing. Perception holds a powerful sway. Ms. Greenwood was convinced that someone connected to her mother's viatical policy had a hand in her death. That was her truth. Billy, whose judgment I trusted, also believed it. McCane was never going to get his nose in this neighborhood to make any kind of assessment. I could walk away and not subject myself to the hassle. But that was the thing about truth and the possibility of it. I had a hard time leaving it alone.

I crossed A1A and turned down a short residential street to a small oceanfront park and pulled into a shaded spot. I stepped over the bulkhead and walked down to the beach. At the edge of the sand you could smell brine drying on the rocks left behind by an out-

going tide. I dug the cell phone out and dialed Sherry
Richards's direct line.

"Strategic Investigations Division, Richards."

"I am surprised and honored not to have your machine answer," I said.

"Freeman. Hey, what happened? The swamp dry
up?"

Her voice had a lilt to it. That was positive. It had
been a few weeks. Maybe she wasn't pissed.

"I had a craving for civilization," I said.

"You're calling me civilized, Max. How sweet."

Still, there was that sarcasm.

"Hey, I'm on dry land. How about lunch?"

"Today? I don't know, Max. Wind's a little stiff.
Might be too busy for you."

I was left again without response. Seriously pissed?
Or joking? Three, maybe four weeks ago we'd been
out on Billy's thirty-four-foot sloop, sailing to nowhere
with Billy and his girlfriend, another lawyer who had
an office in his building.

I had met Richards several months ago. She'd been
on a special task force investigating a string of child
abductions and killings. One of the dead kids had
ended up on my river. Despite myself, I got pulled into
the investigation. She'd kept a professional and wary
distance until the case had broken. Then she'd found
too many reasons for coming to the hospital to check
on me while I convalesced from a gunshot wound.

I tried to see her whenever I came in off the river.
Drinks at a beachside tiki bar. Dinner at Joe's Seafood
Grill on the Intracoastal. I couldn't keep my eyes off

her legs during a Saturday afternoon on the beach. She'd noticed. She was after all, a trained cop.

On the sailing trip she'd surprised me with her dexterity and seamanship. She'd been showing me up from the time we'd pushed off from the dock, but it had only registered a small manly tick with me and probably hadn't even crossed her mind. You don't do much sail trimming on the streets of Philly. Then Billy had decided to unfurl his spinnaker in a downwind run and I'd jumped to show I wasn't useless. The damn sail was huge and far too unwieldy and strange in my hands. When I'd tangled the lines and tripped on a stanchion, the women had smartly taken control. Richards had whipped the lines out of my hands before I went overboard. Then she and Billy's friend expertly set the whisker poles and stood framed in the billowing color and smiled and hooted at the boat's speed. Billy winked at me as I settled back in the cockpit and watched with a tainted respect.

I'd been through a short marriage with a cop in Philadelphia. She, like Richards, had been strong and tough-minded, smart and intuitive. Those were things I liked, things I understood. But both were also emotional, able to absorb a victim's pain, to show an instant empathy. The dual abilities were unsettling.

My ex-wife had also lived on an adrenaline push, one I didn't want to compete for. I still didn't think I knew Richards well enough to know if that was another shared quality. I wasn't sure I wanted to know.

"Oh come on, Max. Don't tell me you got intimidated by two women who could handle a spinnaker in an eight-knot breeze better that you two boys?" she said, breaking my too-long silence.

"Can't intimidate a man who knows his limitations," I said. "And I'm sorry I haven't been in sooner. So introduce me to a new recipe for mangrove snapper."

My apology must have been accepted.

"How about Banyan's at two?" she finally said. "Bring your cash, Freeman, it's on you."

I started back south on A1A, rolled down the windows along a stretch of beachfront where oceanside condos had somehow been banned. From the road the view of the surf and the watery horizon were unobstructed. On the sidewalk I watched a young woman in a bikini walking south, her hips switching like a metronome. Two buzzcut boys walking a pit bull said something to her and she nonchalantly flipped them the finger. I slowed for a middle-aged man crossing from the hotel side, sliding on roller blades, shirtless and tanned with a multicolored parrot perched on one shoulder. I passed a throbbing, low-ride Honda Accord that broadsided me with a bass line from a backseat full of speakers. Eight hours ago I was watching a wild bird hunting gar fish on a thousand-year-old river. Welcome to Florida.

I got off the ocean drive and went back west half a mile, over the Intracoastal bridge, and found a parking spot across the street from Banyan's. Inside the restaurant was an open courtyard dominated by the huge trunk of a live banyan tree that measured some eight feet across and spread its monstrous canopy up and over the surrounding roofs. Its leaves were so dense that even at midday it left a cool and dusky patio below.

When my eyes adjusted to the shade, I saw Richards sitting at a table near one corner, a cop's territory where you could catalog everybody who walked in. She was dressed in a cream-colored suit, white silk blouse underneath. She sat at an angle to the table so she could cross her legs. Even sitting you could see her height in the long bones from knee to ankle and elbow to wrist. Her blonde hair was pulled back. Her eyes, I already knew, would look green today. I am not a smiling man, but approaching the table I could feel it coming into my face.

"Hi. Nice table."

"The advantage of two o'clock lunches," she said without missing a beat. I took her hand and bent to kiss her lightly in greeting and stole a deep draught of her perfume.

"Freeman, you are god-awful thin," she said when I stepped back.

"Thank you," I said, pulling out a chair to the side of hers so I too might have a view.

"What, the fish on the river haven't been cooperative?"

"You mean they don't like to be caught and eaten? Or I'm a piss-poor fisherman?"

"Exactly," she said. "But you're in luck. The special is red snapper, and it's very good here."

I opened a menu as if to make a decision on my own. Took a breath, looked up into her face.

"You're looking fit, detective. Climbing the gears right off that Stair Master?"

One of our connections was a passion for exercise, a shared habit of sweating through a pain we both understood.

Her husband had been a street cop who had died in the line of duty. He had confronted a kid in a holdup and never expected a thirteen-year-old to aim a gun in his face. According to his partner, that night he'd just stared at the barrel and seemed to tilt his head in confusion when the kid pulled the trigger. It was still not long enough in the past.

"No more Stair Master," she answered. "Got a new thing. Aerobics boxing. Great stuff."

"Figures," I said.

She raised an eyebrow, then let the comment slide.

"So, what's up on the river, Freeman? Anything we should know about?"

Her question reminded me how hard it was for her not to always be a cop. There had been some loose ends in the abduction case. A witness, an eighty-year-old legend of the deep Glades, had disappeared and was never found for questioning. The detectives knew he had picked me out as a conduit for special information and wondered if I would ever put them in touch "just for conversation to fill in some holes," they said. What they didn't know was that the old man had saved my life. My repayment was his anonymity.

"Everything is quiet on the river," I said. "But we've got to get you out there again, work on that paddle technique."

"Yeah, sure," she said, but there was a grin on her face.

"No," I said. "This time it's your side of the woods where I think I need some help."

The waiter came and took orders, and as we sipped iced tea, I told Richards about Billy's theory about the insurance scam and murder. I gave her what sketchy information I could about the women's locations and similarities, and about the insurance investigator who, for lack of a better word, was working with me.

She listened, nodding and only interjecting with the proper street names and neighborhood titles. When the fish came, sizzling off the grill and surrounded by dirty rice, we both went quiet.

She finally broke the silence. "Even that many naturals, in that section of the city, wouldn't necessarily raise any flags. And even if Billy alerted us to it, I doubt it would push anyone off the dime to take a closer look."

I looked up from my plate.

"It's a high crime zone, Freeman. You know the drill. Keep the lid on. Try to make insider friends, keep the politics in check and don't sweat the small stuff. They've got bigger problems over there."

It was my turn to raise eyebrows, first at the small stuff comment and then as an unspoken question about the bigger problems. She took a few forkfuls of rice, pulled a loose strand of hair back behind her ears and began again.

She told me about a string of rapes in the same area over the past several years that had also passed across someone's desk. Some were reported, some were just street talk. The women involved were street girls, prostitutes and addicts feeding their habits and not too particular about what they traded for an eight-ball of crack or a dose of heroin.

"They only got reported when the guy got too rough and the women were found hurt. I answered one while I was still on patrol. Girl had marks around her throat like a thick rope had been wrapped around it. She said it was the guy's hands."

That case, like the others, had never been solved. The witnesses were too high to give good descriptions. The crime scenes were either forgotten or so contaminated that they were useless for processing.

She saw me looking at her eyes, watching the way they kept jumping away from mine.

"Goddammit, Freeman. I worked it as much as I could. I was only patrol. I handed it up to the detective bureau."

"I didn't say a word," I said, holding up my palms in defense. She went quiet.

The waiter came back. I ordered coffee and stared up into the canopy of the banyan, following the branches down into the thick mass of tangled roots that formed the trunk.

"So what has changed?" I asked.

"They started turning up dead."

"The rape victims?"

"The users, the hookers, then just women in the neighborhood."

"But not older women?"

"No."

The coffee came and she knew enough about my habit to wait until I'd taken two long swallows.

"So that's their more serious problem? They might have a serial guy out there?" I said.

"We're working the possibility."

Richards declined dessert.

"So when can I get an inside tour?" I asked, taking a chance.

"You're awfully pushy for an ex-cop who's left the job behind him, Max."

"Consider it a favor for Billy."

She looked into my face again. A grin pulled at the corners of her mouth.

"OK. I'll consider it as such. I'll have to get a waiver for a ride along, but your name is not exactly unknown. You do remember Chief Hammonds?"

Hammonds had been in charge of the abduction case. We did not hold a mutual trust.

"I would never hold either of you responsible if something should happen," I said.

A long moment passed. "Tonight then," she said, catching me off guard. "Meet me at ten in front of the office."

She got up, bent to kiss me on the cheek and walked away before the bill came.

"Thanks for lunch."

I watched her from our back table vantage point, heels clicking on the flagstone, never looking back so I could see if there was a smile on her face.

9

I called Billy's office. He listened to my description of the meeting with Mary Greenwood and then my lunch with Richards.

"What's with you two? Maybe we should get out for a sail again, heh?"

"No."

I refused to let his silence lead me to say more. I waited him out.

"She have anything to add?"

I told him about the rapes and murders in the area where his dead women lived.

"She's going to give me a tour of the zone late tonight. All right if I wait it out at your place?"

"I'll call Murray at the desk and I'll bring some take-out," he said and clicked off.

I took A1A north, through the condo canyons and past blocks of motels and businesses catering to the tourist crowd. On occasion there would be a stretch of thick green only interrupted by iron gates guarding driveways that twisted up to the backs of beachfront mansions. The huge flat paddles of sea grape leaves billowed up next to the road and twenty-foot high fans of white bird-of-paradise twisted in the wake of the cars. I passed a landscaping truck, mowers and string trimmers being loaded in the back by a crew of men. I thought of the whiskey-laced conversation I'd heard between three old dockside fishermen. One night they were betting on how long it would take the prodigious Florida ferns and vines and water plants to sprout through all the asphalt and concrete and reclaim the land if there were no humans here to cut it back.

"Thirty years and it'd be back to the high tide line," said one.

"Hell, fifteen," said another.

"No more'n ten."

The argument went on but not one of them ventured that it couldn't be done.

Billy lived in a new beachfront high-rise. I'd stayed with him there during my first few weeks in South Florida. His penthouse apartment was spacious, decorated in expensive natural wood and hung with collected art. His pride was the curving wall of glass that faced out over the Atlantic. The wide porch was always bathed in fresh salt air. The only sound was the low hum of wind nibbling at the concrete corners and the brush of breakers on the sand below. It was the exact opposite of everything Billy had grown up in.

I parked my truck in a visitor's spot out front. Inside the ornate lobby, Murray greeted me at the desk. Murray was a trim, balding man who always dressed in a suit and tie and spoke with a clipped and efficient English accent. Billy once did a computer dossier on him and discovered Murray had been born and raised in Brooklyn. But if quizzed, he could give you the specific walking directions from London's Hermitage to the Suffolk House and estimate the time it would take to get there based on the gait and stride you used crossing his lobby. He was a sort of concierge and security man for the building. The residents paid him well.

"Good day, Mr. Freeman."

"Murray. How you doin'," I said.

"Mr. Manchester has called ahead. Please do go up, sir. I shall unlock the doors electronically."

"Thanks for the lift, Murray."

Ever since Billy had told me about the Brooklyn thing I'd had to stifle the urge to mock his accent. Instead I'd just try to get a rise. It never worked.

At the twelfth floor the elevator doors opened onto Billy's private vestibule. The double doors to his apartment were of dark wood. The carpet was thick. The flowers in a vase against the wall were fresh. I heard the electronic snick of the lock and went in. The air was cool and sanitized. The place was immaculate and like always I found myself moving through it like a visitor in a museum. I went straight to the open kitchen and started coffee brewing. Then I slid open a door to the patio and stood at the rail, my nose into the wind.

The sun was high and white and the wind had set down a corduroy pattern on the ocean surface. From this height the varied water depths showed in shades of turquoise, cerulean and then a cobalt blue that spread to the horizon. The narrow strip of beach had shrunk since the last time I'd visited. The tide and wave action had eaten away at least fifteen yards. I didn't relish the idea of doing three miles in that soft sand. The thought of it made me lean into the rail and stretch my calves. But some of my best grinding came while I was running or paddling, and it was going to take some grinding to determine where to go with Billy's dead women.

I went to the guest bedroom, found some running shorts, a T-shirt and the running shoes that Billy held here for me. I changed and poured another cup of coffee, and carried it to the rail. The wind was stiffening. I swung a heel up on the rail and stretched. Bent. Counted. Swung the other leg up.

Would someone kill old women for money? Of course.

How would he know who to kill? Inside job. List of names.

Do it himself, or contract it? Money guys don't do the dirty work.

How does the racial angle fit? It might never fit.

I still wasn't sold on the whole premise and now I was bringing Richards into it. It was how conspiracy theories were started. Look out, Oliver Stone.

I put my palms on the floor, propped my toes on the seat of the chaise lounge and did fifty pushups. The blood was singing in my ears when I stood up and exhaled. I took a deep swig of coffee. Time to plow the sand.

10

Eddie felt the cop car turn around. He'd watched it pass, keeping his head down, pushing his cart, willing himself invisible. But after the green and white prowl car had passed by he heard the wheels slow and then crunch the stone, first on one shoulder and then the other. He heard the U-turn and now he thought he could feel the heat of the engine on his back.

The chrome bumper pulled even with him, then the green fender, then the white, smiling face.

"Hey, junk man," said the young officer in the passenger seat. Eddie said nothing.

"Wassaaaaap?" the officer wailed, his tongue sticking out, his partner grinning.

Eddie had heard the blatting before, followed by laughter. He wondered why only white people did it.

"I do not know," Eddie answered and stopped his pushing.

The prowl car stopped with him.

"What you got in the cart today, junk man? Anything in there you shouldn't have?"

Eddie had talked with the police before. Most of the time they left him alone. They never hurt him. The one time he'd been arrested was for burglary when they found a half dozen potted plants in his cart. He'd just picked them up out of someone's carport. He was planning to sell them but the police stopped him and said they were stolen. They took him in when he said he didn't know where the plants came from but promised to put them back. He had no money for bail, so he spent sixty days in the county jail.

Eddie didn't mind jail. The food was good and after a few days they put him on a special floor the guards called the forensic unit. That's where Eddie met the doctor. They'd had some good talks. The doc had taken care of him.

All the guards were good to him and he did whatever they told him. One day a prisoner had broken a toilet and a work crew came to bust up the porcelain and chip out some of the concrete. They filled a huge trash can and the guards laughed when two of the workers couldn't drag it away.

"Eddie," the guard called out. "Come carry this out into the hall for these gentlemen."

Eddie put down the mop he'd been using and walked over. He bent and gripped the sides of the can and hefted it up onto his chest and walked it to the hall while everyone stared. He'd lifted heavier things. The guards smiled and were even nicer to him.

Another day a prisoner started screaming in his cell,

crazy like, threatening to burn up his mattress with a pack of matches. He was strong and wild. The guards told him to throw the matches out but he spit at them through the bars instead. Two of them looked at each other and then the one said:

"Eddie."

It was the guard that was always asking Eddie for help. "Go in there and get the matches, Eddie."

The guard sat at his desk and listened to the heavy thumping, the sound of bone against bars and thick muscle against concrete. Eddie came back out with the matches and put them on the desk.

"Thank you, Eddie."

"Yessir," he said. Eddie had crushed the bones of a strong man's hands before.

"You don't have anything in that cart from Sue and Lou's Restaurant, do you junk man?" The young white officer was still talking, but neither he nor his partner had gotten out of the car, and Eddie knew if they didn't get out of the car it was going to be alright.

"Because somebody helped themselves through the back door over there last night," the officer said.

Eddie knew. He'd been through that alley and saw the busted lock on the door but he had pushed on by. No need to get caught up in all that now.

"I do not know," Eddie said.

"You do not know, huh?" the young officer repeated. "That might be the truest statement I've heard today."

The officers looked at each other, proud for some reason of their words. "You be cool, junk man," said the partner as they pulled away.

Eddie watched until the taillights disappeared and then pushed on.

"I know lots of police," he whispered to himself. "I talks to them all the time."

Eddie reached deep into his pocket and fished out the watch that he never wore on his wrist. He checked the time. Now he was late.

He turned down Twenty-ninth and quickened his pace. The cart rattled over the rough macadam. At Sunrise Boulevard he scanned the busy street. Rush hour. Working people leaving downtown on the east side heading west to their nice homes out in the suburbs. They kept their eyes on the cars in front of them. They stopped only when the red lights held them. It was like a train moving through an ugly patch of landscape and no one on board cared about the view.

Eddie's eyes were on the Bromell's Liquor Store across the street. It had been there since he was a child, sitting back off the main road, a broad parking lot on two sides. Even when they repainted the outside of the building some new yellow or purple color, the walls always seemed dingy, the dirt and grease somehow seeping back through the fresh color like a weeping wound through a bandage. Its present color was an odd orange, like a Mexican cantina, Eddie had heard someone say.

The young ones were hanging in their usual spot next to the pay phones. Yapping. Calling each other nigger and laughing at whoever it was today that had to be picked on. The older men pulled up in their Buicks or the Cadillacs with the sprung bumpers, limped in and came out with bottles in paper bags.

The working men arrived in pickups with the shiny toolboxes in the truck beds. Eddie remembered when white boys with a Confederate flag pasted in the rear window were the only ones who drove such trucks. The world had changed.

Finally Eddie let the front wheels of the cart down off the curb and pushed his way across four busy lanes of traffic. No one honked. No one jammed on their brakes or cussed out the window. Eddie was invisible.

At the far edge of the parking lot he stood in the shade of a sprawling willow and waited. Without looking up he saw everyone who entered and left, matched them with cars, noted their clothes, paid particular attention to their hands: big or fine boned, stuck down in pockets or dangling at their sides.

When the bronze-colored Chevy Caprice pulled in, Eddie watched the man get out, sweep the area without stopping his eyes at the willow, and then stride into the store. Once he was inside Eddie moved.

The Caprice was an old model but flawless. Not a rust spot or a dent. The paint was unblemished. The chrome sparkling. The whitewalls brilliant and unstained. The license plate was multicolored and decorated with stick figures of playing children and said, "Choose Life."

Eddie took up a position on the sidewalk in front of the car and leaned against Bromell's cantina wall. The young ones paid him no mind, an ol' trash man.

While he waited, Eddie watched another car pull in and park in the back of the lot, near his willow tree.

The car looked like a cheap rental. The white man backed into the space, the way a cop might. Eddie kept his head down, peering up through his eyebrows. The ones at the phone nudged each other and under his breath, one hissed "Five-Oh." Eddie knew it meant they'd spotted a cop on the street. Their voices got softer but they didn't move. One of the pay phones rang and they let it jangle eight times before it stopped.

Eddie watched the new car. The outline of the man's head looked huge and Eddie thought he could almost see his eyes. Then he watched the man lift a bottle wrapped in a paper bag to his lips and take a long drink. It wasn't a cop. Just another drinking man.

Eddie's own man came out of the store. He was wearing a short-brimmed touring cap. A package was under his arm and as he passed, Eddie watched his hands. The fingers were pale and thin and cupped. Eddie unfolded his own massive palm and the man dropped a tightly rolled package into it and Eddie's hand snapped shut like a jaw. The man got into his car and only tried to make eye contact after he was behind the wheel. Eddie kept his brow down and pushed away as the Caprice backed out.

No one noticed the exchange or no one cared that a white man had dropped some change into an old black junk man's hand. Eddie jammed the roll down into his pocket next to the watch and moved north, across Sunrise, up Twenty-third and through an alley. He did not hurry, but he did not break stride until he reached the old warehouse where they used to park the city buses and where the mechanic crews had left the packed dirt black and flaky with spilled oil and engine fluids. Back behind a rusted Dumpster, he stopped, swung his head north to south, and satisfied he was alone, dug out the roll and loosened it.

Three hundred-dollar bills and the white notebook paper, the kind with the blue lines and the thin red stripe on one side. Typed in the middle of the page:

Mrs. Abigail Thompson
1027 NW 32nd Ave.

Eddie knew Ms. Thompson from years past. She may have even gone to church with his mother. He also knew the alley behind her house. Eddie knew all the alleys.

11

Billy poured himself another glass of Merlot. I took another swallow of coffee. Both of us had had enough shrimp fried rice. I was ready for a prowl car tour of the area where Billy's women had died.

The beach run had been painful. The humidity of surfside Florida teamed up with the soft sand to make my three miles a fine torture. Most of my life my regular runs had been done on Philadelphia streets, several blocks east to Front Street and then north along the Delaware to Bookbinders and back. I was used to cruising on hard concrete, slapping a rhythm, dodging through intersections. If I went down the shore, I'd do miles on the Ocean City beach at low tide when the sand was wet and brown and hard. Here it was slogging, half your energy used digging out of each footstep. My lungs were burning but I'd sprinted the last hundred yards down in ankle-deep water.

The shower afterwards was always a treat. Out at my shack all I had was a rain barrel above my porch that was fed by water flowing from the eaves and fitted with a hose and nozzle.

Billy filled me in on his paper trace while we ate. His women had come to South Florida at different times and they'd bought their insurance policies at different ages but all within a close time period. They probably knew one another because of their era and proximity, but it would have been on a social basis. None was in business with the other. There were no family connections. No shared churches in the recent past.

"Has McCane been any help to you?" I said.

"He has accessed s-some dates and m-medical questionnaires on the policies his company h-held."

"You talking with him?"

"Only on the phone."

"I'll check with him tomorrow. Maybe I should have asked him along tonight."

We traded sideways glances.

"Maybe not," I said, and we both relaxed.

I pushed the plate away. I'd already bagged my things, planning to get back to the river afterwards. I'd dressed in jeans and a dark polo shirt and black, soft-soled shoes.

"How is Sherry?"

"Looks good," I said.

"W-When are you two going to quit d-dancing around each other?"

Billy was trained to be forward and blunt. But he rarely took that step with me.

"She's still got a ghost in her head."

"She's the only one who's b-been able to p-pull you off the river."

"Liar," I said, fishing out my keys.

"Well, I d-don't count," Billy said.

I drained the coffee and tipped the cup at him.

"Yes, you do."

When I got to the sheriff's office I parked my truck near the front entrance and was starting across the lot when a spotlight snapped on me. When I raised a hand to shade my eyes, the light went off. Richards was backed into a spot and was behind the wheel of a green-and-white. I opened her passenger side and climbed in. She was in uniform. Starched short-sleeved white shirt and deep green trousers with a stripe down the leg. Her hair was pinned up. Her 9mm in a leather holster at her side.

"Regulation," she said. "Got to wear the whole rig if you're driving a squad car," she said in greeting.

"I remember," I said.

She slid a clipboard over to me with a form on top.

"Absolves the office if you get hurt. Sign the bottom."

"I think you've got the wrong impression of me and my propensity for getting hurt," I said.

"No, I don't," she answered, grinning as she shifted into drive.

We pulled onto the street and headed west. The strip centers were single-story and second-rate. A carpet outlet. A fish market. "Jiggles" nightclub with "Girls, Live Girls."

We turned north onto a side street and a block and a half off the main thoroughfare we were into residential.

There were no sidewalks but street lamps were set every two blocks. At this time of night cars were parked in most of the driveways, some on the grassless swale. Richards punched off the headlights and swung onto another cross street. Two houses in she twisted the handle on the door-mounted spotlight and snapped it on. The beam caught the black maw of an open doorway and she swept across the windows that were boarded up with plywood.

"Crack houses," she said. "We try to keep them boarded up. But they rip the stuff down faster than we can get it up. The owner who lives god knows where won't keep it sealed even if it is the law."

She flashed back over the doorway and the light picked up some movement inside.

"You arrest them for trespassing or possession and they're out by Friday."

She flipped off the spot and pulled the headlights back on and kept going. As a patrolman in Philly I'd done the same thing. It was exactly the same neighborhood only one-story instead of two. Less brick. More trees. Same despair.

"Your husband work this zone?" I asked and immediately wondered why the question came into my mouth.

The dash lights gave her jawline a sharp edge. Her nose held a small but not indelicate hump. A touch of mascara showed at the corner of her eye, which stayed focused ahead.

"Sometimes," she finally said. "But he preferred the eastern zones. He wasn't much for the action. He worked a lot with kids in the Police Athletic League."

And got shot by a kid, I silently finished the sentence for her.

She turned another corner.

We rolled through an intersection and Richards slowed again to a crawl. Every city has a dope hole and this was theirs. Nearly eleven o'clock and there was a busy nonchalance that showed in the slow spin each man did as the green-and-white slid by. Drag from a cigarette. "I ain't give a shit about no cop," but the cupped hand helps hide the face. The older ones sitting on empty milk crates, elbows on knees, something too interesting to stare at in the dirt but proud enough to raise their jaws in defiance as the back fender glides by. The young ones who don't hide. They goof and throw signs with twisted fingers and pull at the loose fabric in their crotch and their eyes say "Ain't no big thing" and their justification is "All I'm doin' is bidness."

We got some extra scrutiny; two new faces on the night shift. But I knew Richards wasn't showing me this for the dealers. Dope dealers don't kill old ladies for life insurance money. They also don't need to rape and murder. There are enough addicts who will give it up for whatever the dealer wants. Richards was looking past them, into the back corners and at the side of houses for the desperate ones.

"We tried to set up surveillance, watch the customers drive in and out, check the plates, run the names through NCIC looking for a hit with a sex crime conviction. Nothing.

"We've got some liaison with the community leaders who are trying to clean things up, appealed to their sense of safety, hoping to pick up at least some rumor. Nothing."

"Too scared?"

"And distrustful," she replied.

"And scared," I repeated.

"And probably tired as hell of nothing ever changing."

She tightened her jaw and we turned again. She seemed to have a destination in mind. A few more blocks and we pulled to a stop next to a dark, undeveloped field of overgrown grasses and brush. The orange glow of the street lamps had little effect on the interior of the empty land.

"Not exactly an urban park," I said.

"The land was originally bought by the city for some kind of trash transfer station," she said. "But the commissioner who represents this area fought it. So now they're waiting for someone to come up with the money to develop it."

"Been waiting long?"

"Years."

She flipped on the spotlight and swung it into the darkness. A few tree trunks took shape. A clump of saw palmetto. A squat bunker of gray concrete with a single black window.

"This is where we found the last body," she said,

reaching down to grab a long-handled flashlight and her riot baton. "Take a look?" she said.

It wasn't really a question as she popped open the door. I got out and as I walked around she closed and locked the car, leaving the spotlight on. I followed her into the brush.

"The report came in on a pay phone back up near the dealer's corner. First time that line has been dialed to the police station. Patrol and a rescue responded. Girl had been dead eight, ten hours."

I was watching Richards's feet, following in her tracks, wishing for a flashlight of my own.

"She was ID'ed through fingerprints. We had her on file for some minor possession charges, loitering. She was basically a heroin addict. Her sister kept kicking her out and taking her back in."

Richards unsnapped the holster of her 9mm as we approached the bunker, stepped around the wall and found the doorway. Inside the squad car's spotlight painted a square on the wall opposite the window. I stepped in and the stench hit my nose and made my eyes water. It had been a while, but the reek of stale sweat, rotting food and wet mold was not unlike some corners I'd had to stick my head in down in the Philadelphia subway tunnels. Richards's flashlight beam sprayed across the walls and into all four corners and then settled on the mattress.

"They found her face up, skirt pulled up and top pulled down around her waist, just like the others. This one had fresh bruises on her ankle and one wrist."

"Toxicology?"

"She was high but the twist in her neck and the bruises around her throat were so obvious they knew before the M.E. got here she'd had her windpipe crushed."

Around our feet there were half a dozen empty plastic lighters strewn among the trash. Pipers, I thought. When I was a young cop my Philadelphia sergeant had been standing with me at a magistrate's walk-through at the roundhouse and he grabbed the shackled hand of a guy in line and twisted his thumb up for me to see.

"Bic thumb," he called the clubbed and thickly callused digit. "From spinning the lighter so many times trying to keep the crack lit."

I reached out and pushed Richards's light back to the mattress. Stains and burn marks and ripped fabric where the rats had gnawed holes.

"You guys ever consider taking this thing to the lab for a DNA sampling?"

"Jesus, Max. You want to type every scumball and user in a fifteen-block radius? They're all in there somewhere," she said. "A defense attorney would have a field day."

She had a point.

We got back to the car and she unlocked and switched off the spot, started the engine and kicked the A.C. up.

"That was the third of the most recent ones," she said, reaching into her backseat and bringing out a bottle of water. Then she reached back again to get a thermos.

"Coffee?"

"You're a mind reader."

"Doesn't take much," she said and I watched her take a drink and then continue.

"The victim before that was in a stand of bushes near the overpass. One before that was in an abandoned press box at the high school. All the crime scenes were places that the addicts know and use. But nobody's come forward with credible information, even the confidential informants looking for a few bucks."

"Maybe even they're afraid," I offered, pouring the coffee into the plastic top of the thermos.

She was staring out into the orange glow on the pavement ahead.

"They're never more afraid than they are hungry."

We cruised the area for another hour, down a handful of alleys, up behind an old style drive-in theater where movies were flashing away on three different giant screens and along a street that she called the border. Even in the dark you could see that on one side of the street were modest but well kept homes, trimmed grass, planted palms and nice sedans in the drives. It was, Richards said, a neighborhood where middle-class blacks had come together to make a stand and a community. On the other side of the street were the scrub-and-dirt yards, the lot with two broken cars alongside the drive, the open lot with a pile of discarded sofas and trash.

"Don't ask me how you get from one side to the

other," Richards said. "Smarter people than me have been trying to figure it for a long, long time."

We drove back to the sheriff's building and pulled into a spot next to my truck. Light from the poles all around poured in through the windshield.

"So that's the nickel tour," she said, turning off the ignition and unsnapping her seatbelt.

"I appreciate the time," I said.

She leaned back into the corner of her seat and door. The light had an odd way of playing in her eyes. Sometimes they were a light gray, sometimes a deep green. The shadows in the car kept me from seeing them now.

"So."

"So?" I could feel her grinning at my awkwardness.

"You staying at Billy's tonight?"

"No. I need to get back out to the river."

"Ahh. Back to the frogs and gators."

"Yeah, well," I said, my time to smile. I let the moment sit for a while. "Billy says we're dancing, you and I."

"Billy's right," she said.

"So am I dancing too fast, or too slow?"

"You're being very careful, Max. I like that in a man."

She sat up straighter in her seat. The onboard computer was between us. She raised her eyebrows to the building façade, as if she needed to remind me where we were.

"See you later, officer," I said.

I popped the handle on the door and started to put the thermos down in the seat.

"Why don't you just take that with you for the ride back," she said. "It'll keep you company."

"I'm not sure when I'll get it back to you."

"I'm guessing soon enough," she said and I watched her eyes, trying to find the color.

"OK," I said, stepping back and closing the door.

12

I pulled into the ranger station parking lot at 4:00 A.M. There was a single light on over the washhouse door. Another burned high on a pole over the dock. When I wheeled into my usual spot, my headlights hit a small reflective sign: PARKING BY PERMIT ONLY.

I sat staring at the words, looked around stupidly like I wasn't sure I was in the right place, and then felt the blood rising into my ears. I put the truck in reverse, punched it and sent a spray of shell and dirt clattering through the undercarriage. I backed into a spot on the other side of the lot, clearly in a public space. I pulled out my bags and locked up. As I approached the pool of light near the dock, I saw another sign that was staked next to my overturned canoe: ALL UNATTENDED WATERCRAFT ARE THE SOLE RESPONSIBILITY OF THE OWNER. THE PARK IS NOT LIABLE FOR ANY LOSS OR DAMAGE.

I flipped the canoe, checked for the paddle, still safe inside, and then dragged the boat to the ramp. I stored my bags and turned back to stare into the front of the ranger's office, hoping to catch the new man, maybe at the window, awakened by my rumblings. Nothing. All I could see was a single red dot glowing inside; a security alarm indicator that had never been there before.

I pushed the boat forward and floated the bow. With one foot in the stern and hands gripping either gunwale, I shoved off onto black water.

I took several strokes west and then sensed the incoming tide taking me. I could feel the water through the thin hull like a shiver under a horse's coat. A half moon was pinned high in the sky like a flat silver brooch and its light glittered on the calm water. I cleared my throat and spat once, then started paddling toward home. The moon followed.

It took me more than an hour to reach my shack, and the thin light of dawn was already seeping into the eastern sky. I checked the stairs and went up. I stripped off my clothes and stepped back out to stand under the rain-barrel shower and used a few gallons to hose the sheen of sweat off. I pulled on some shorts and poured the rest of the thermos of Richards's coffee into a mug, then sat in my straight-backed chair and put my heels up on the table. By the third sip I was asleep.

I dreamed of O'Hara's Gym, down on Cantrell, east of the school. O'Hara's son, Frankie, had been a friend since we were boys. It was Frankie who invited me to the gym one day after football practice and let me spar with him. His father didn't mind teaching a little to someone from the neighborhood, and after they found out I could take a decent shot to the head without going down, they didn't mind having a six-foot-three, 215-pound sparring partner around for the real fighters to warm up on.

I just liked the place. The heat in the winter. The odor of liniment and sweat and talcum. The rhythm of leather slapping on leather and the sting and whoosh of a jump rope. That and the silence.

No one in O'Hara's wasted their breath on words. A trainer might yelp instructions to his fighter in the ring, or have a low conference between the two-minute bells, but a man on the heavy bag didn't trash talk. A guy rattling the speed bag only breathed swiftly and kept the rhythm. The shadow boxers had nothing to say to the man in the mirror.

I'd been going to O'Hara's for a year before my father found out. On a November evening one of his patrol buddies led him and another cop in after their shift. They'd stopped off at Rourke's Tavern like always. They came in yapping.

"I'll show ya. It's true," said the smallest of the group. Schmitty, I think they called him.

"Bullshit," my father was saying, and the sound of his voice turned me just as I was climbing into the raised ring to take a few rounds with a middleweight trying to tune up for a bout that month in Atlantic City.

Mr. O'Hara walked over to the trio, and even though they had changed out of their uniforms, he knew from their carriage and sense of ownership who they were.

"Can I help you officers?"

By that time my father had spotted me. His seventeen-year-old son up in the ring, without his knowledge, or his permission.

"That's his kid there," Schmitty said, touching my father's arm and pointing up at me.

Mr. O'Hara looked into my father's face and then back at me as if to confirm the resemblance.

"Yeah. OK. Nice to meet you Mr. Freeman," he said. "You want to watch your boy, OK."

My father had a look on his face that I'd never seen, a look of surprise, but with the narrowed eyes of his constant skepticism and an alcoholic sheen of disregard.

The bell for the round rang and snapped my eyes off his. From the other corner, Mohammed "Timmy" Williams came bouncing across the ring. Williams was a professional and had an agenda. He moved like mercury spilled from a bottle, slipping, circling to his right, body bunched but fluid and within itself. I tried to cut off the ring on him like Mr. O'Hara had taught us but Mohammed was much too fast, bouncing on his toes, automatically anticipating the moves that I had to think about. It was like trying to pinch that ball of silver liquid. You could never seem to touch it. He slipped in close and fired two left jabs into my high right glove. The first one I blocked, the second I hadn't even realized he'd thrown. The punch knocked my headgear askew. Now I circled and shot out a jab, just to be moving.

"Atta boy, Maxey." The one called Schmitty was yelling.

"Long arms," quietly rasped Mohammed's trainer from his corner.

The professional was there to work technique. His upcoming opponent was long-limbed like me. He was trying to perfect his ability to slip inside those long punches and punish the other fighter's torso.

I was there to get hit. It's what sparring partners do. I kept my elbows down and in, knowing his intent. He fired two more jabs that snapped into my headgear, high on the forehead.

"Come on, Maxey. Give 'em a shot."

The cop named Schmitty was excited. The rest of the gym was, as usual, voiceless. My father only watched.

I threw another, instinctive left jab that Mohammed deftly stepped into and let slide by his ear before delivering a short right hook to my exposed ribs. My mouthpiece came halfway out onto my lips from the air that popped from my chest. My knees lost the connection between upper and lower legs for an instant and I stumbled back. Mohammed bounced away and waited. I tried to get my lungs to work again. We circled again. Mohammed started to throw stinging punches, combinations, left-right, left-right off my headgear.

"Come on, Maxey," yelled the cop. "Give some back to this homey."

I heard the machine rhythm of the speed bag lurch, just once, before regaining its patter. I heard someone on the heavy bag snap it with a vicious punch.

Mohammed moved back in. His punches to my head were too quick to stop but that was not his intent. Despite that knowledge, my elbows were instinctively coming up. He dropped his guard suddenly and I took the bait, delivering my own combination. This time he slapped away my left, slipped under my right and hooked two short punches, filled with the power of his hips and legs, into my midsection, just above my hip bones.

I lost my eyesight for a second and had a strange recollection of the first time I tried to stand on ice skates as a child and felt no friction under my feet.

When my vision returned and refocused, I was down on the canvas with my knees together and ankles splayed out, squatting. Mohammed was back in his corner, standing, taking instruction from his trainer. The room was still spinning when I turned to look out of the ring. My father was missing. And then I saw his back turned to me. The sight of his son being dropped to the floor by a black man, even in sport, was something he could not bear to witness. His shoulders filled the door to the street and he met the cold wind without dropping his chin.

13

The light woke me. A midday sun left bright and clean by a high pressure system that had swept the sky clear of cloud. I was not used to sleeping in daylight.

"The evils of city nightlife," I said aloud, with no one to share the joke. I got up and set the coffeepot going and rummaged through the rough pantry shelves for canned fruit and a sealed loaf of bread. As I ate I could hear the hard "keowk" of a tri-colored heron outside, working the tide pools on the western bank of the river. I looked for a book in my sloppy stack on the top bunk and picked a collection of stories about the Dakotas by Jonathan Raban. I took it outside and sat on the top step, propping my back against the south wall. I was deep into the fourth story when the cell phone started chirping.

"Yeah, Billy?" I said instinctively into the handset.

"Ya'll wait till I say hello an' you wouldn't make

that mistake," McCane said from the other side of the connection.

"McCane?" I said. "Who gave you this number?"

"Well, that'd be your pal Manchester. He doesn't seem too eager to deal with me one-on-one, if you know what I mean."

I could hear a tinkling of glassware and the strains of a Patsy Cline song in the background.

"What do you need?" I said.

"I need to get with you on this little purchase group I've been sniffin' out, Freeman. Why don't you come join me? We'll sit down and have a drink and sift through it a bit."

"Why don't you sift through it over the phone? I'm afraid I can't make it back in today," I said. It was early afternoon and I could hear the softening of the hard vowels and drawn out *s* sounds in McCane's speech, telltale patterns I'd heard too many times in my youth. He wouldn't be sober by suppertime.

"Okay. Have it your way, bud," he started. "We got a bit of a trail working here. But it's not exactly clear where it's leadin'. Through our company I pulled some private documentation and laid out the purchases on our insured. Then I got some friends with the other companies to do the same."

He was clicking back into business mode and I had to admire the transition.

"Now, these investment boys pull these life policies in from a lot of places. The so-called gay community was a choice target when that AIDS thing was knockin' 'em off a few years back. And there wasn't too much illegal goin' on, since these boys figured they had a death sentence anyway so let's get the money and party. Hell, the investors bought 'em up for twenty cents on the dollar. The boys spent the money while they shriveled up, and when they died, the investors cashed out."

Even with a few drinks in him, McCane still only bordered on displaying the homophobia in his voice. Nothing that an e-mail or printed deposition would ever show.

"But the money guys needed a go-between," he continued. "They sure as hell weren't gonna go hang out in the boy bars themselves recruitin' business."

"So you're saying there's a go-between here also?"

"There's always a go-between Freeman. You know that. The money men, especially the white-collar money men, never get their hands dirty."

McCane sounded more bitter than he had a right to, considering he worked for the white-collar insurance world. But he was right. No different than the drug trade or Internet scams. The guys with the investment capital never saw the streets. They sat high above, just doing business.

"So you have a line on any of these middlemen?"

"I've got an eye out, Freeman. And you ought to, too. Your boy Manchester is pretty good at trackin' the financials on whatever names I give him. I'll just follow the money trail."

McCane took a long pause. I could almost hear the whiskey sliding down his throat.

"How much money do you pay a man to kill old ladies in their beds?" I finally said.

"Depends on the man, Freeman. Depends on the man," he said. "So what have you got for me, Freeman? I assume you ain't leavin' this all to me."

I told him about my tour of the neighborhood, my meeting with a local detective I knew and the suspicion that they had a serial rapist who had progressed to choking his victims to death. Whether it had any connection with our case, I wasn't sure. Hell, I wasn't even sure we had a case. But if I believed what McCane was telling me, he wasn't just dismissing it.

"So you're with me on this?" he repeated.

"You stay on the middlemen, McCane. Leave the locals to me," I said.

I hung up and sat on the top step of my porch and watched a heron fishing in the shallow waters under a stand of pond apple trees. The bird's roving eye seemed to be everywhere at once, but I knew it was focused on a target. The tapered beak was always poised. I sipped from my cup and watched the filtered sunlight dance around him and then, with a flick, the beak struck and came up with a small pilchard fish pinched at the head, its tail flapping furiously. Nice lunch, I thought. But instead of flying away with its catch, the heron stood frozen, its eye still worrying. I looked up into the canopy, scanning the top foliage, then twisted around and saw him. The big osprey was perched in the top of one of the twin cypress trees that marked the entrance to my shack. He was looking down at the heron, or perhaps at me as if to say, "Now that's how to catch a fish."

After a minute the standoff ended. The heron finally

bent its legs, unfolded its wings and took flight. The osprey didn't move. He sat there, as if waiting for me to decide on a course to take. I stared at him for a few minutes, then got up and went inside, closing the door softly behind me.

14

This one was not as weak. Eddie replaced the metal lid on Ms. Thompson's garbage can in the alley behind her small house on Thirty-second Avenue. Inside there had been empty packages from frozen dinners, the smell of shaved pork from a wad of tin foil and a confetti of small ripped pink packages of sugar substitute. It was not like the garbage he'd seen on earlier forays. The others had eaten little or nothing. Their cans had been near empty, holding only mounds of tissues, a few half-filled cans of protein substitute and bags of medical trash. Ms. Thompson was not waiting on the edge.

Eddie knew she lived alone. Her husband was long dead. But he had seen her move about in the past. Had even watched her drive that old Chrysler till just a couple years back. She was more like his own mother, feisty and bitchy and always getting on him about how he needed a job. Humpin' 'round all day pickin' trash and bein' laughed at by everyone in the neighborhood ain't no job, she would say. And why don't he clean hisself up and go on Sunday with her down to Piney Grove Church like he used to and her not thinking that was twenty-five years ago when he was still a boy. No, this one would be more like his momma, who wouldn't get off him, constantly pushing on him about making money to help her out and how come he can't be like other sons and what was he going to do when she was gone and where would he stay and who would take care of him then. Well, today he had three new hundred-dollar bills in his pocket down by his watch and he was making it just fine in her house without her. No, this Ms. Thompson would not be as easy as the others. She'd be more like his momma.

He watched the house from the cover of a ratty hedge. The smell of the alley didn't bother him. A trail of ants led from one of the trash cans to the base of a shed across the way. Their industry was constant. It was an odd, jiggling ribbon of life that would only be temporarily interrupted when Eddie slapped his boot down, crushing half a dozen. Then he would again study Ms. Thompson's window lights, marking her habits. He'd push his cart up and down her street. And by the time he came back, the ants would have resumed their marching. Eddie wondered what would happen when a car or truck rolled through the alley and mashed the whole line.

On the third night, the lights in Ms. Thompson's kitchen went out and Eddie moved. In the darkness he could get closer. He left his cart and took up a position in the side yard. He inspected the grates on the side windows. He knew he could quietly turn those bolts out if he had to. And usually, if he removed the iron grate and set it down on the lawn, the window behind it would be carelessly unlocked. People didn't care, Eddie thought. They set themselves up for what they got.

He moved again, to the other side of the house into a shadow on the neighbor's wood slat fence. He could see the carport from here. The old Chrysler looked like it hadn't moved for years. The windshield was layered with dust. The tires had gone soft and there were cracks in the rubber whitewalls. His eyes moved to the carport door that led into Ms. Thompson's utility room. It was a louvered door, the dull metal handle and lockset still strong, but there was no grate over the windowpanes. With a couple of panes out he could reach through and snap open the lock.

He waited for an hour. Never dozed off. Never once did he lose his concentration on the inside noises. He saw when the living room lights went off and then the shine of the small bathroom window on the back lawn. He waited that one out, too. Eddie was patient, but the stiff hundred-dollar bills in his pocket seemed to press into his thigh. He needed to see the Brown Man.

When the house had been dark for another hour, he stepped to the carport door and slipped the socks over his hands and started on the jalousies. With his hand inside, he turned the deadbolt and slipped the chain—he would have to remember to refasten it when he left. Inside the small laundry room, the odor of bleach stung his nostrils. He moved, a single wary step at a time. A clock ticked on the kitchen wall. The hallway was carpeted and quiet. The bedroom door was ajar and the bathroom across the hallway smelled oddly of what? Cologne?

Eddie gripped the door, fingers wrapped around its front edge, and pressed it up and tight against the hinges to avoid any squeaking as he eased it open. He was surprised to see a line of light glowing at the bottom of a door inside. Another bathroom. It was wrong for this neighborhood. She must have had it installed, Eddie thought. He had never seen a second bathroom in these houses. He watched the strip for several seconds, soaking up the light, adjusting his eyes. In the high-mounted bed, he could see the line of Ms. Thompson's body turned away from him. He could see her white hair in the slight glow. Another pillow lay next to her, punched down and indented. Eddie picked it up, assessed the position of the old woman again, and then pushed the material over her face.

He was just beginning to close his eyes to her muffled groans when light burst into the room.

"Abby baby, you purrin' like a ol' lioness ain't too tired . . ." The man coming out of the lighted bathroom caught a glimpse of the huge thick back bent over the woman he had just recently started calling his girlfriend and yelped "What the hell? . . ."

The speed of Eddie's left hand swapped its hold from the woman to the old man's throat before another syllable could be uttered. The man's eyes went big.

Eddie's right palm remained on the pillow and the light from the doorway caught all three of them in an ugly instant of time.

Just as the old man started kicking Eddie tightened his grip, feeling the soft flesh and then crushing the bony windpipe under his thumb. He spread the fingers of his other hand and kept the pocket of his huge palm over the mouth of the other. And he silently held the pose, watching the man's face go from red to dusty blue in the light of the new master bathroom. Eddie was a patient man and did not move until he was sure that the lives in both of his hands were gone.

15

I was upriver on a rare morning paddle when the cell phone chirped from my bag in the bow of the canoe. I'd been up with the sun. Found it impossible to read and was actually pacing the wood floor of the shack when I decided to grind out a trip to the headwaters. The water had been high and the morning light spackled the ferns and pond apple leaves that crowded the edges. The river twisted and folded back in on itself and if you stopped moving, the deep quiet and moist greenness could sweep even an unimaginative mind back several millenniums. In the morning light I'd seen several glowing white moonflowers nestled in a small protected bog, and I knew that back in a thicket at the end of one offshoot stream were a half dozen undisturbed orchids. By luck no one had found them. But like a hundred years ago, when exploiters of the delicate flowers had plucked them from the dark hammocks of the Everglades until they were nearly extinct, there was little optimism that these few would remain hidden.

I'd spent more than an hour plowing up past Workman's Dam and on to the culvert where Everglades water from the L131 Canal poured into the river to give it an extra flow. I had pulled the canoe up onto the grass bank and was on top of the levee looking out over acre upon acre of brown-green sawgrass. The view extended to the horizon like unbroken fields of Kansas wheat. The only break was a dark clump far in the distance that looked like bush but was actually a hammock of sixty-foot-tall pine, and mahogany and crepe myrtle rooted in high ground in the river of grass.

The bleating of the cell phone in my canoe spoiled the quiet. I loped down the bank to answer it and Richards was on the line.

"Hey. Nice to hear your voice on such a great morning," I said, sounding too chipper.

The silence on the other end dampened my enthusiasm.

"I don't know how the hell you do it, Freeman," she said. "But you've got one special nose for trouble."

I was back in the world, outside another low-slung home on the northwest side. The address Richards gave me wasn't hard to find. Three patrol cars and a crime scene truck were still parked at haphazard angles in front. A black, unmarked Chevy Suburban was backed into the driveway.

The uniformed cops were on the front lawn keeping a small gathering of people back. A black officer with a bald, shiny scalp was bristled up in front of a group of three black men. All their voices, even the cop's, were ratcheted up to a high pitch.

"What you mean they investigatin'?" said one. "Shit, they ain't done no damn investigatin' the last time. Hell, they ain't investigated nothin' on this side of town, an' you know that's true."

The cop had his hands spread out in front of him, as though the paleness of his palms facing the group would settle them.

"I know. I know. I hear you," the cop was saying. "But you got to change some things from the inside, fellas. You know what I'm sayin'."

I asked one of the other officers for Richards and as I was led up to the front door the knot of men shut down their conversation and watched me. They were the same three I had seen at Ms. Greenwood's mother's home.

"Comin' through," someone in the doorway said, and I turned as a black vinyl body bag was taken out on a wheeled stretcher. The eyes of the crowd followed it to the back doors of the Suburban. I followed the cop into the house.

No one was in the living room. A sectional couch sat against a wall of frosted mirrors. An expensive looking crystal clock was in open sight on an end table. Crime scene techs were working in the kitchen, spinning small fat brushes dipped in fingerprint powder along the window casements. Outside on the patio Richards was sitting at a table across from an elderly black woman who was chastising the detective as if she were a dull schoolgirl.

"Young lady, I have toll you and seven more of you all, no. I did not struggle. I took me a gasp of breath when I heard George go to chokin' and spittin' and I laid myself still. I didn't even breathe until that pilla eased up on my face and then I still didn't move. I knowed what was comin'. I didn't just come in from the fields young lady. I know what these mens want."

The woman looked at me when I reluctantly stepped out of the house. Her eyes stopped me. She'd seen too many men in her house in the last few hours. Richards turned and nodded at me and I took a step back and waited.

"So you just laid still and fooled him?" Richards asked, turning back to the woman.

"I don't know about fooled," she said. "Only one been made a fool is me. I stayed still. Left that pilla on my face and prayed to the Lord. Then I felt him put George down next to me. He covered him up like he was layin' him to rest and I guess he was.

"I heard him leave and I still laid there, not movin' a muscle, a dead man next to me. But I knows when to keep my head down, young lady. An' when to get up and holler and that wasn't no time for hollerin'."

The woman turned her head and looked down at the empty tabletop. A single tear formed at the corner of her eye and then rolled down her cheek and disappeared into the wrinkles of her face. For some reason, it seemed out of place to see an old person cry. My own mother had always hidden that aspect of her sorrow.

This woman was unashamed.

"When I was truly sure he was gone, I called y'all on nine-one-one," she said, still not looking up. "And I waited right on the bed, watchin' after George."

Richards let it go, touched the back of the old woman's hand and got up quietly. Back in the house she crossed her arms in front of her. I put my hands in my pockets.

"The first guys on the scene had to take down the front door to get in," she said. "Luckily, it was an experienced patrolman who checked the other doors and windows first and eyeballed everything. The place was tight. No signs of forced entry."

She must have seen the frown on my face. "You saw the burglar bars on the windows?"

"And the deadbolt and chain on the front door," I said.

"The utility room door leading to the carport is the only other entry not covered. The bolt was tight. Even the chain was hooked. But the crime scene guys studied the shit out of it this time," she said, and I could see her eyes taking on the grayer cast that came with either anger or challenge.

"The clips on the jalousie panes, four of them, had recently been bent out, and then back."

"Which means he put them back?"

"Carefully. Took his time. Had to figure both of them were dead and he had time to cover."

"Jesus."

I thought about Gary Heidnik in North Philly. Heidnik was a self-styled minister who'd been abducting mentally handicapped women for years and keeping them chained in his basement. When police finally discovered his "house of horrors," they found one woman still alive and body parts of another in his freezer. Each day his neighbors saw him. Each day he carefully locked up his house to go out. Each day, careful and meticulous like a business.

"So that's the husband?" I asked, hooking my thumb to the body bag. "It doesn't fit my guy's motive or yours, going after a couple."

"Boyfriend," she said, and she couldn't keep a sardonic smile from pulling at the corners of her mouth.

"Excuse me?"

"George Harris is, was, Ms. Thompson's boyfriend. He lived three blocks away. A widower. She'd been seeing him for about a year." Richards was flipping through a narrow notebook. "Younger man. Seventy-four."

Ms. Thompson was closer to eighty. She was in the same generation as the others on Billy's list. Her living arrangement didn't bother me. It was the change. If this was meant to be part of the string, the guy had screwed up on his surveillance. Which meant he was slipping.

"So the killer comes in, thinking she's all alone and gets surprised?" I said.

"Ms. Thompson says George was very discreet," Richards said, but her eyes were past me, caught by something out past the front window.

Outside one of the cops was having an arms-crossed discussion with two black women on the curb. One already had her hands up on her hips, not a good sign.

The other was trying to see past him, as if just a glimpse of her friend inside might change the mask of worry on her face. I turned back to Richards.

"So, have you got anyone on the paper trail? The insurance?"

"That's why you're here, Freeman," she said. "You and Billy already have an inside track on that. You could find out a hell of a lot faster than we could. If it fits with your theory, it's a whole different case. But I'm not going to bring this whole idea to Hammonds without a more solid connection."

She was a good detective, willing to look at the long odds if there was a possibility, but smart enough to play the game by the book. It was something I had never learned.

"Give me Ms. Thompson's date of birth and social security number and we'll work it," I said.

She was already tearing a slip from her pad, and looking back outside.

"Thanks, Max," she said, moving now to the front door.

When she left I wandered back through the house. It had the same feeling as Ms. Jackson's, a place caught in the past. High school graduation pictures of the grandkids, propped up to form a small altar on the console TV. A threadbare runner over the worn carpet in the hall. Hand towels, faded with age, snapped around the handles of drawers. I kept my hands in my pockets and went into the utility room. The scene techs had dusted the door casings and all of the jalousie panes. They'd left smears of black powder on the white enamel of the washer and dryer. But there was something in the air, an odor that wasn't an old person's. It wasn't a detergent or bleach smell. It wasn't the sweat of men gathered here to do their technical work. There was one small window in the room, sealed and barred and facing the backyard and the alley behind. I stood staring and closed my eyes and took a full, deep breath into my nostrils. It was the smell of the streets, the subway passage deep below Philly's City Hall, the heating grate after midnight at Eleventh and Moravian, the pile of stained and oily blankets piled around the homeless guy a block from the bus terminal on Thirteenth, and the acrid odor at the brick shack only a couple of miles from here.

I could feel it in my nose and it was a smell that did not belong here.

On my way out I passed Richards, who was escorting the two black women from the curb to the back patio where Ms. Thompson still sat. She pointed them in a direction they already knew and turned.

"You alright?" she said looking into my face.

"Yeah. I'll call you when I get something," I said. "Your guys check the alley?"

"Of course."

"Nothing?"

"Trash. Why? You expect anything?"

"No. Not with this guy," I said and walked away.

Back in my truck I called Billy at his office. I gave

him a rundown on the overnight killing and the information on Ms. Thompson.

"I'll start as much of a paper chase as I can," Billy said. "But you're going to have to get this over to McCane."

"Yeah. I'll page him next," I said. "I already owe him a call."

Billy, as usual, was right. McCane's resources would be better and faster than even he could get out of public records, though it wasn't a collaboration I relished. Billy listened to my silence.

"Are you turning into a believer yet?" he asked.

"Maybe."

"And now we've got a survivor."

"But she didn't see a damn thing, Billy," I said in frustration. "There was a pillow over her face the whole time."

"Max. Max," he said, waiting for my attention. "I didn't say witness, Max. I said survivor. Survivor is a good thing."

16

I beeped McCane. Punched in my cell number and waited. My truck cab was hot, the glare of the sun snapping off the hood and windshield. Out in front of me the trio of men I'd seen earlier had taken up a position across the street in the shade of a tree. I started the truck and kicked up the A.C. My cell chirped.

"Freeman. How you doin', bud? Thought maybe you forgot about me son, and right now, you don't want to be forgettin' me."

"I can't imagine you're the kind of guy who's easy to forget, McCane."

In the background I could hear music. Maybe it was the same song that had been playing before. Maybe McCane hadn't moved from his seat at the bar.

"I've got another name for you to run through your insurance sources," I said, expecting a skeptical grumble.

"Yeah? Well start talkin', cause all you're going to be

117

doin' is listening when you get here, partner. We got us some fat to chew."

McCane gave me directions to an address on the east side, and as I rolled down the street the neighborhood posse of three was watching me. All three turned their heads as I passed and I couldn't be sure, but it looked like the head man tipped up his chin.

I drove to a commercial strip in the city. This time of year the shopping malls and restaurants were doing a brisk business. The closer to the ocean, the brighter the building facades, the more commerce ruled.

I was looking for a movie marquee on the right and then a turn into a plaza. Kim's Alley Bar was deep in the corner and I found a space in the lot several doors down and walked back. Inside the stained-glass door I had to stop and let my eyes adjust to the dimness. It was a small place, split in two by a hip-high wall that separated a lounge area from a bar that ran the length of the back wall. There were four men sitting on stools. As my sight sharpened I saw McCane at the far end, a sheaf of papers spread out in front of him, an empty shot glass and a half-drunk shell of beer within reach.

As I crossed the distance a young, perky bartender called out a greeting, as if she'd just seen me yesterday. As I came closer I saw that she was standing in front of the most handsome hand-carved wood and beveled glass bar back I had ever seen. I was still staring when I got to McCane's side. The dark wood was intricately scrolled at the ends and across the high façade. Tiers of glass-fronted cabinets were stacked up, and they framed three individual mirrors. It had to be a century old, a stunning piece in this place where everything outside was new and sun-brightened and faux tropical.

"Suzy. Get Mr. Freeman here a drink, darlin', so's he'll have somethin' to put in that open mouth of his."

McCane pushed back the stool next to him with the toe of his shoe and I asked Suzy for a dark ale in honor of the place.

"Nice, huh?" McCane said, matching my sight line to the woodwork before us. "They say it was imported from some place in New England somethin' like fifty years ago in pieces and put back together here. Somehow makes you feel at home even if you ain't never had anything like it at home."

Suzy brought me an ale in a tall, thick glass and I took a sip and had to agree. McCane just pointed at his glass and she topped him off.

"So what's with the new name, bud? We got ourselves another dead ol' lady?"

"Old man," I said and his eyebrows raised. "The woman lives six blocks north of the last one. She survived but the way it went down, I think the killer thought he'd finished her."

"Dead guy came in and saved her?"

"No. Looks like he was already there, sleeping with her."

McCane just snorted and shook his head.

"Breaks the pattern," he said. "But not a bad way to go."

I took a longer drink of the ale and in the ornate mirror I saw a wide-shouldered, rangy-looking man with a tanned and weathered face. His hair looked bleached from the sun and his forearms were lined with cabled muscle as he held the tall glass to his face. I did not have a mirror in my shack. The eyes I saw staring back at me over the rim of my glass looked somehow changed to me.

"So the old lady got a look at this suspect?" McCane said.

"No. Her face was covered with a pillow he was using to smother her. So we got nothing. Might not even be connected," I said. "But it feels right."

McCane seemed truly disappointed, and took another drink.

"All right, bud. But we got bigger fish to fry now."

He filled me in on his middleman theory. He and Billy might not be able to look each other objectively in the face, but their paper chase had become an effective partnership.

Billy had run down the legal work on several of the insurance policies. In the ways of lawyers and accountants, there had been a meticulous recording of money expended in obtaining the discounted policies.

One of the line items was the payment of a finder's fee. Billy had come up with a Dr. Harold Marshack, psychologist, address in Florida.

"Guy lives in a condo by the beach," said McCane. "Gives the same address for his office. Manchester ran him through some Internet link he's got with the state department of transportation and gave me his plate and car description and I tailed him."

McCane finished off his shot. The small glass looked ridiculous pinched between his thick fingers. There was no alcoholic glow in his eyes. Just the enjoyment of letting his tale leak out slowly to me.

"I followed him to the grocery for milk and donuts. To the Office Depot for paper and stuff. To the bank. Then he takes me on a squirrelly ride to the west side. At first I thought he'd made me. But he was just being careful."

McCane took another drink of his beer chaser.

"He makes one stop at some shabby liquor store on the edge of blacktown over on West Sunrise."

No one at the bar acknowledged the slur, if they even heard it. The bartender kept washing glasses. The two guys watching ESPN never flinched. Bonnie Raitt kept singing about shattered love on the jukebox. I'd been wrong about the lack of effect the alcohol was having on McCane as he continued.

"He goes into the store empty-handed. Comes out with a bottle in a bag, gives a handout to some pan-handler and goes straight back home."

"You get anything from the store clerk?"

McCane pointed again at his empty glasses. I waved Suzy off.

"I came back. Old Tom in the store pretends like I'm not even there. Then when I started asking him about Marshack, he gives me some shit about 'White cop askin' bout some white guy in here? That's a new one.' And then he goes on about how Marshack comes in maybe once every couple months. He buys a bottle of Hennessy Cognac. Doesn't use the phone or meet anyone. Just buys his booze and leaves. Only weird thing I could get out of the old coot was that the good doctor always pays with a hundred-dollar bill. No doubt an oddity in that place."

McCane waited a moment to let the information settle and then asked, "That ring any bells for you?" He was looking intently into my face for an answer.

I was trying to grind out the scene in my head, working the possibilities. There was a new rock in there but with only the slightest edge to it, and I couldn't get a hold of it.

"You on him again last night?" I finally said.

"I found a nice comfortable spot across the road from his place. Watched the Caprice for hours. Never moved."

"What time did you leave?"

"I woke up at 5:00 A.M. You know how surveillance goes. But the Caprice was still there. I even moseyed on over and felt the hood. Stone cold."

McCane was a bigot. Might be an alcoholic. But he hadn't lost all of his cop instincts.

"He ain't your doer, Freeman," he said. "Not the kind who creeps into houses and smothers old ladies. I seen him up close. He ain't got the hands for it. But if you get your detective friend to get a warrant and toss his place we might find something."

I stopped and let McCane's words settle in my head for a few seconds.

"Which detective is that?" I asked, knowing Billy would not have brought Richards's name into a conversation with McCane.

"Guy like you gotta have a local on the pad, Free-man. No P.I. I know gets along without one."

He held my eyes with his and didn't allow them to slide away. I didn't respond.

"You track the Thompson policy if there is one. We'll wait and see what we come up with," I said, pushing back the stool and taking one last appreciative look at the bar back.

"Follow the money, bud," McCane said, tossing back another shot. "Just follow the money."

17

Eddie went home when he got confused. And now he was home. He'd come in at night, through the back using his old key, and sat down in the middle of the living room floor and listened.

It wasn't the old man suddenly coming out of the bathroom that confused him. It was bothersome. Bothersome that someone else was with Ms. Thompson and he hadn't known. But the old man's neck was weak and Eddie could feel the rickety bones inside and it really hadn't taken much effort. Afterwards he'd been careful to lay the old fella out and slipped out quiet. He'd even remembered the chain before he put each glass pane back in its place.

No. That part had gone all right. But then he'd waited, just like he always had before, at the post box on Seventh Avenue and Mr. Harold never came by and now he was confused.

Mr. Harold always brought the rest of the money after it was done, an envelope with cash and a date written on one of the bills so Eddie would know when to meet him again at the liquor store. But Eddie waited at the mail drop box at the far end of the parking lot and Mr. Harold never showed. The old Caprice never pulled up and he never dropped the envelope in Eddie's hand instead of in the box. Eddie waited until the security guard finally came out and told him to get the hell off the property, it was federal land and what the hell was he doin' there anyway. And Eddie answered, "I do not know."

That's what had confused him. What had he done to make Mr. Harold not come? What had he done wrong? Ms. Thompson was gone like she was supposed to be. The old man was just extra. Eddie had tried to figure it out by going down to the Brown Man's and buying another bundle. He'd gone over to Riverside Park and done the heroin until dark. But he ended up here, back at his mother's house.

He sat listening for her now, facing the kitchen. He had stuffed the towels from the bathroom under her door. He'd used the gray duct tape ("best damn thing ever made for fixin' ") and sealed all the cracks. He'd done the same on her closet and inside all the windows in her room. He'd done a good job and he didn't want to see it again. So he sat with his back to her door and listened. Momma had never stopped tellin' him what to do. Now the least she could do was help him figure out what to do next.

I drove back north on I-95, heading to Billy's apartment, where he said he'd been working on another case but couldn't keep his head out of the insurance and murders he was convinced were connected. On the main interstate through South Florida you are best off being a lemming. You fit yourself into one of the middle lanes and then stay in time with those in front of you. If they do seventy, that's what you do. If they crawl at thirty-five, you join them. There will always be someone faster, more impatient, more aggressive than you. Let them, I reminded myself.

At Billy's I waved at Murray and he raised one eyebrow in return. Upstairs Billy hit the electronic lock and when I came in he was at the kitchen counter, starting coffee.

"I also h-have beer if it's not too early. Help yourself. I still have s-some work," he said, going back into his study. In his working room Billy had two computer systems, one almost always connected to local, state and federal government sites. The walls of the room were lined with law and reference books. He is a workaholic, a trait I did not envy.

I got a beer. It wasn't too early. I unscrewed the cap and walked out to the balcony through the already opened glass door. Billy's abuse of A.C., I believe, was a spiteful reaction to his years growing up on the broiling summer streets of North Philly. In the summer only Mustafa's Groceries had air conditioning through one rattling wall unit. You could go over to Blizzard's Billiards on Fifth Street and take a chance at getting your ass kicked by whatever gang controlled that corner. But Billy had stayed home instead with a fan set up in his second-story staircase window and read.

I drank half the beer with two long, breathless swallows and the cold spread up into my cheekbones and made my eyes tear. Out on the horizon a soft string of bruised clouds was piling up. The late afternoon sun gave them color. The washed out shades of gray, purple and pink looked like a child's watercolor spread with too much moisture. I sat back on the chaise and thought about the first time I'd seen both my and Billy's mothers together.

My mother had been working at the First Methodist Church on Bainbridge and Fourth Street in the historic section. For her own reasons my mother had left her life-long Catholic church in South Philly, and every Sunday she took an early bus ride to First Methodist. Since my father had never stepped foot in church since his confirmation, it was not a subject he cared about or controlled her with. At the church she would work the kitchen, setting up coffee and rolls and morning juices for the clergy and their assistants. Because it was a volunteer position and a 6:00 A.M. requirement, she was mostly alone. I had already joined the police department and had come with her to help before, but when we arrived this day there was a stout, black woman in the kitchen. She had on an apron and was setting out heavy white coffee mugs.

She greeted my mother by her first name and with a meaningful hug. When I was introduced she offered her hand and said, "Oh my, Ann-Marie—this can't be the boy you been talkin' bout. Why, this is a man!

"Son, you is twice the size of my boy Billy."

I looked at my mother. Her face was prideful and soft and more comfortable with this woman and their morning embrace than I had ever witnessed at home among blood relations. Their friendship would not have been easy in either of their respective neighborhoods, but it had a simple existence in this church basement. It was also a secret friendship that I admired because I knew my father would never have allowed it. That she had moved behind his back gave me a special appreciation for her.

In the weeks and months to follow I would see them several times in that kitchen, laughing together over a sink of dishes or huddled with their hands cupped over one another's at the long empty table.

One winter morning I had come to pick her up, and when I came down the steps the two of them were whispering to each other and didn't notice me. At first I thought they were praying, their hands again clasped together on the table.

But this time I saw a small bottle being passed, short and made of brown glass like an old apothecary bottle. And this time the tears had not been wiped away from my mother's face. When I looked at Mrs. Manchester's wet eyes she bent to my mother and whispered, "It's all right, baby. The Lord will forgive."

My mother refused to tell me why she had been crying. As far as I knew she had never let loose the demons in her life to anyone save a priest or her own version of God. She was quiet for the entire trip home but when I helped her out of the car and to the stoop, she turned to me and said, "You should go to Florida, Maxey. Mrs. Manchester's boy Billy is a lawyer down there. You should meet him. You could leave this behind." Then she spun with the back of her hand turned up to me, her sign of enough said, and stepped up into the house.

"M-Max?"

Billy was standing next to me. A glass of white wine was in one hand and a sweating bottle of beer in the other.

"You are absorbed."

"Thinking about old times," I said. "And mothers."

"Ahh," was his only response.

Billy and I had spent many nights on this porch, hashing out our mothers' scheme. When the pieces were put together, he'd understood his own mother's burden of complicity, and I had a clearer grasp on gratitude.

We both looked out at the ocean. Three miles out it was raining. I could see the dark curtain slurring down with thick bands falling in curls.

"To old times," Billy said, raising his wine. We touched bottle to glass but neither of us drank.

"Our investors are t-taking us on quite a ch-chase," Billy said, interrupting the thought.

Billy had been tracking the investors. He'd run their incorporation records back through the state's Bureau of Professional Regulations. He'd found three companies filed under fictitious—but not necessarily illegal—names. He'd finally found the names of corporate officers, but none of them had raised any red flags.

"Just incorporated b-businessmen. We can follow the t-trail of money that maybe p-puts McCane's middleman in direct contact with them. But it's still a hard case t-to make."

"Invisible," I said, more to myself than Billy.

"In m-many ways, yes."

"And if all our theories are correct. They still might not know what's going on with their money?"

"Oh, they know w-what's going on with their money," Billy said. "This kind always knows w-what's going on with their money."

18

I stayed in Billy's guest room, on clean sheets and in air conditioning. I had drunk too much, and the good old bad times kept swimming in my head. Once I woke up shivering and pulled a blanket up from the foot of the bed. I curled up like a child and fell back into an old and recurring dream of the night my father died.

I was working patrol on the B shift. It was 5:00 A.M. and my mother had probably sat as long as she could while the daylight crept in and pushed the dark out of their room. When she could see him lying there, she couldn't stand it any longer and called.

The sergeant got me on the radio and asked me to meet him at the roundhouse. I figured I'd screwed up again on some paperwork, until I saw his face in the dispatch room. My uncle Keith, another lifetime cop, was standing next to him.

"Let me drive ya home, kid," Keith said.

Eighth Street was slick with morning rain when we

made the corner at Mifflin. Porch lights and street lamps were still reflecting on the sidewalks and the wet hood of the M.E.'s van double-parked in front of my parents' house. I still had my uniform on and the beat cop, who I only knew in passing, took off his hat. On the porch next door Mrs. O'Keefe stood with her fingers curled over her mouth.

I walked in the front door and past the stairs and down the narrow hall where I knew I would find my mother, sitting at the kitchen table, dressed in her flowered day dress, staring up at the east side window like she had done every morning since I could remember. Her hands were folded like a supplicant praying to daybreak.

"Mom?"

"Maxey?" she answered, turning from the light. I pulled a chair across the wooden floor and sat in front of her and took her hands in mine.

"You okay, Mom?"

"I'm fine, Max. Just fine now."

There was not so much as a glisten in her eyes. Her face was drawn and sallow, but no more than it had been in the two years that the old man had been sick. He had gone weak fast since a liver ailment had pulled him down from his hard-drinking, anger-spitting heights. He'd been on disability with the department. Several months ago, when they'd tried to appease his hate of hospitals by bringing an oxygen tank and mask into his room, he'd slapped the offending thing away and cursed the technician until the guy slammed the front door.

But my mother remained vigilant, always with the homemade soup that he demanded. Always within earshot of his denigrating orders, and frequently still within slapping distance of his hand.

As we sat there I heard the creak of the loose wood on the third step from the top of the staircase, and I winced at the sound—and saw my mother blink also. How many times had we both heard that creaking step and held our breaths, lying in our beds hoping his anger would not visit us?

When I was young, and he came to my door first, I would cower and cry and could only wish him away and then cover my head with the pillow to drown out the curses and accusations that would inevitably come and to ward off the open-handed blows. Then when he left I would keep the pillow over my ears to shield the noise from down the hall, where a hardened fist and my mother's stifled cries bit into the night. When I got older, I wished him to my door and engaged him with a measured defiance, in the hope that at least some of his energy would be spent before he went to her. When I was fourteen I took a handful of nails and pounded them into the riser on that third step. But it never stopped the warning sound.

This morning it was my uncle's weight coming down from where his brother lay dead that creaked the stair. And like his brother, Uncle Keith's broad build filled the kitchen door. My mother looked up, dry-eyed, into his face.

"You alright, Ann-Marie?"

"Yes," she said and I felt her hands flex once under my own.

"Max boy. You wanna see him once upstairs before they take him out?"

"No," I answered.

He didn't react, knowing enough not to say more.

"Then I'll take care of it, Ann-Marie," he said, crossing the kitchen floor and laying a hand on her shoulder. She reached up to pat his back and he pressed a small brown apothecary bottle into her palm.

"So you take care of this. OK?"

I was up early. Billy had already started coffee and was practicing his morning ritual with the paper. We apologized for our respective hangovers and I went down to the beach for a run to purge my pores and memories.

When I got back, sweat-stained and vowing to do more than two miles next time, Billy was on his way out.

"There is f-fruit blend in the refrigerator and S-Sherry called," he said. "T-Tell her I appreciate w-what she's doing."

I reached her on her cell and arranged to meet her at Lester's Diner.

"Just trying to fatten you up, Freeman," she said. She had some paperwork that she needed me to see. When I wondered out loud why we couldn't just meet in her office, she knew I was needling her.

"Sure. Come right up and say hello to Hammonds.

He'll be thrilled to hear you've got your fingers in another one of our cases."

When I pulled into Lester's it was past noon. There were several pickups and a couple of truck tractors in the parking lot. Lester's was built in the tradition of the old Northeast railcar diners. Long and rectangular, the outside was lined with windows. Inside, chrome swivel stools were lined up at the counter. There were three rows of booths upholstered in slick red vinyl. Richards was in the last booth in the corner, sitting on the bench facing the door. She was dressed in jeans and a buttoned blouse and she had left her hair down. Papers and what appeared to be a city street map were spread out on the table. As I slid into the seat opposite her she took a few stray strands of hair and tucked them behind her ear.

"Nice choice for a workplace," I said.

"Might as well be an annex," she said. "Sit here long enough and you'll see nearly every patrol officer and detective on two shifts."

The waitress came, dressed in a dingy, '50s-style white uniform that looked like it might have been new when she was young.

"Can I get cha, hon?"

I couldn't help smiling, waiting for the gum to crack. Richards picked up on the grin.

"Julia Palamara. Max Freeman," she said in introduction. "He'll have coffee."

"Pleasure," the waitress said.

The coffee cup was heavy, ceramic and huge. Julia left a brown plastic pot for refills. I liked the place.

"So here's the stack of rape and homicide files, all of them grouped in the same general area and going back ten years," Richards started. "No fingerprints, a hodgepodge of DNA in only the recent cases, and statements by the rape victims that are sketchy, incomplete and pretty damn vague considering.

"I mapped the locations all out on here," she said, spinning the map to face me. "The cases we looked at are red, then I stuck your list of what were classified as naturals in green."

The circle that enveloped twelve different spots from the high school press box to the concrete bunker to the Thompson house was way too tight. I just looked up at her and then took a long sip from the deep cup.

"It was spread over time," she said, her voice sounding defensive. "They weren't all linked together, and considering the neighborhood . . ."

I still said nothing. And then she quit, too. Julia came back and gave us both an excuse to stop staring at the map and avoiding each other's eyes. We both ordered breakfast.

"OK," I started. "Let's assume the women fit in with the others, just for now. Do that and you've got three motives; sex, violence for the sake of violence, and money."

"Wrong, Freeman," she said, tightening up her voice. "You haven't been out in that shack that long. Rape isn't about sex. It's all about violence and control."

"OK, OK. Agreed," I said. "If we're going on the theory that your guy wasn't just after sex that got out of hand and that's why you've got some victims still alive."

"Still violence, Freeman."

She was looking full into my face, her eyes a pewter gray. I couldn't hold them.

"OK. You're right," I admitted.

"Good," she said. "Now, tell me again where the money comes in other than to your so-called investors, who sure as hell aren't out here in their three-piece suits killing clients."

I told her about Billy's paper chase, how he'd come up with a possible middleman, some guy named Marshack, who was connected with a finder's fee. I also told her about McCane and how the insurance investigator had tailed Marshack to the liquor store. When I pointed out the location on the map, it fell just outside her circle.

"And you say the only thing he got from the store clerk was that the white guy with the Caprice comes in once every month or so? That's pretty thin, Max," she said. "I know the place isn't much for white clientele. But how come the clerk even marks this guy?"

"The hundred-dollar bills," I said. "Guy always pays with a clean hundred."

I started to pick up my coffee when she reached over without a word and cradled the big cup in her hands and took a sip.

"So you're thinking this middleman has found somebody in the neighborhood who already doesn't mind killing to do the old women, quietly and carefully?"

"And get paid," I said.

"And never leave a clue?"

"In a place where people aren't looking too hard for clues," I said.

"Careful, Freeman."

Our plates came with omelets and hash browns and buttermilk pancakes. We talked about the possibilities as we ate. Would the theoretical killer have to be local, someone who knew the area? Or an outsider doing good surveillance?

"Get out of South Philly, Freeman. Hard to see some big white Italian sitting in his Chevy watching those houses very long without somebody noticing," she said. "Despite what it looks like, we do run patrol down those streets. And especially in the drug areas they're going to stop any suspicious white guys who might be buyers."

"OK," I said. "So he belongs there," I offered. "He's a local."

She took a couple of bites. Thought about it.

"Someone who stays a lot to himself because you know how word gets around," she said. "He's not somebody who's going to be out bragging about it, or some cop's informant would have used it by now."

"True," I nodded.

"So what does this hit man do when he isn't killing old ladies, or if we lump them, also raping and strangling streetwalkers and addicts?" she said.

"Maybe he's buying things," I said, the thought coming to me. "With hundred-dollar bills."

The grinding was starting in my head, but it was new, something I'd have to roll around to get the size and shape of. She took another bite, then reached over and stole another sip of my coffee, leaving a trace of lipstick on the cup. I brought the coffee cup to my own mouth and she watched me.

"You know, you're not too bad at this cops and robbers stuff. You ever think of coming back? I mean down here, not Philly?"

Unconsciously my fingers went to my neck and touched the circle of soft scar tissue.

"Yeah, I might have thought about it," I said and then let it go.

"Hell, Freeman. I might even write you a recommendation." And there was that smile again.

She gathered up her paperwork while I paid the bill. As we left she was stopped by officers coming in.

"Hey, how's it going, Sherry?" Or "Detective. Long time. You mean they let you guys out for lunch?"

Each one of them nodded at me, maybe waiting for an introduction, maybe just sizing me up, trying to place me into a category. It is something cops do. I was doing it, too.

Outside I walked her to her car. She stopped before opening the door.

"You know why I like you, Max?" she said, pulling my attention to her eyes. "Because you're careful."

The question must have risen into my face. It was the second time she'd brought it up.

"You're careful because you see the bad possibilities in everybody."

I couldn't think of a response.

"Call me on my cell," she said. "We're sharing here. Right?"

"Yes," I said, and walked away.

19

I drove back toward the northwest, heading to Ms. Thompson's house with a purpose that wouldn't pan out without the right people. And it was there that I'd last seen them.

When I rolled past the front of her house only the carport door still held the yellow crime scene tape across its threshold. At the next corner I turned back south, this time using the narrow alley. Behind the Thompson house, I stopped and got out, assessing the way a stealthy man on foot might have approached. The alley-side street lamp was a jagged cone of broken glass.

From here he would have been able to see the windows of the back bedroom, but not the front, where Ms. Thompson might have discreetly let her man in.

I sat down on an upended paint can and watched the back of the house, guessing at the difficulty a killer would have getting across the darkened lawn to the storage shed behind the carport. None. A trail of ants worked in a line across the breadth of the alley like a fishing line on the surface of nervous water.

He could have sat back here for hours. But who might have seen him? Trash collectors? Kids on their bikes? Neighbors using the alley to park instead of circling for a street-side spot?

I moved the can closer to the hedge and estimated the cover he would have had in the dark to work on the carport door. Behind me I picked up the sound of shoes scuffing to my left. They weren't sneaking, just walking slow and sure, like athletes showing up for practice.

The three young men I'd first mistaken for the neighborhood drug posse had gathered behind me. The one who seemed to be the leader was watching me with a curious head tilt. The other two had cut off any escape route to the north. My truck clogged the path to the south. Their hands were out of their pockets this time. One of them was wearing a thin black glove with the fingers cut off. It was impossible to tell with their baggy, calf-high shorts and long shirts whether they were carrying or not.

They let me check them before the leader took a couple of steps closer and then squatted on his heels to bring his face down even to mine.

"This part of the investigation, G?"

He had put a derisive emphasis on the "in" syllable.

"I'm not with the government," I said, holding his eyes but watching for movement from the pair behind him. I could probably kick through him and scramble for the truck. But if they were armed, I wouldn't make it.

"This the second place you showin' up after somebody did wrong in the off-limits," the leader said. "Ms. Mary said you was helpin'."

It was a statement, and it is my practice not to answer statements that are phrased as questions. Some people think I'm a smart-ass when I do it.

"I'm working with an attorney," I answered. "A friend of the women who have recently died like Ms. Mary's mother."

"Workin' on what? Takin' they money?"

His eyes betrayed no anger in the accusation. They only drifted off my face to the direction of the Thompson house. He was three feet away. I could see the two gold caps on his back teeth when he spoke. His breath was odorless.

"Some people don't think those women died naturally," I said. "Some people think they might have been murdered for their life insurance money."

"Family gets insurance," he said, this time his voice held a sense of dismissal.

"In these cases, some investors bought up the policies. But the longer the women lived, the less the policies were worth."

He kept his eyes on the house for several beats, assessing my words.

"Ms. Thompson ain't dead," he finally said, finding the flaw in my explanation.

"Some people think whoever's doing the killing didn't know she was being visited by Mr. Harris."

One of the two standing close behind now snickered, and the sound pulled at the corner of the leader's mouth.

"Hell," he said. "Everybody know Mr. Harris be visitin'."

When the leader went quiet, the others followed. He shifted his feet and the movement made me flinch, but I covered by asking my own question.

"What did you mean by 'the off-limits?' "

He assessed me again and decided to answer.

"They's parts of the neighborhood that business ain't done," he said. "People here know you don't mess in the places where the old folks live. 'Specially the great-grands."

The two behind were nodding.

"You wanna sell and smoke some shit, they's a place for that. We don't mess with that. They leave the off-limits alone."

I nodded my head. It was an odd truce, but admirable in some way. Again the silence had its time.

"I think the man who's killing the elderly women, including Ms. Mary's mother, is somebody from the neighborhood."

He again gave me the head tilt.

"I see," he suddenly said, changing the mannerisms in his voice to a mocking, officious tone. "Once again it is the notorious black-on-black crime pattern."

I started to think I'd made a mistake in tactics, trying to turn him into a source.

"Look, this guy knows the streets, the layout of the homes, the habits of the people," I said, trying again. "You know how a stranger would stick out here. You're the first ones who would see it. Maybe this guy is someone who moved in years ago, started to fit in."

The leader was staring again at the house, thinking.

"Maybe it's somebody that flashes money around. Acts like everybody's friend so no one suspects," I said.

"He got his needs?" the leader said, catching me off guard. He saw that I didn't understand.

"You know, habits. Dope, women, gamblin'?"

"Hundred-dollar bills," I said, dropping the only signature I had.

Now it was his turn to be confused.

"If he's got habits, he might be paying with hundred-dollar bills," I said.

The leader looked around at his boys. They shook their heads. He turned back to me.

"You got a cell or somethin'?" he said.

I gave him my cell number. He didn't write it down but I got the impression he didn't need to. He stood up and so did I. He was four inches shorter, but the difference didn't seem to phase him like it did some men.

"We'll see, G," he said and then turned and walked away, the others following. Their hands were all back in their pockets, and when they got to the end of the alley they turned left and headed west.

I stayed in the neighborhood, driving, watching, grinding the possibilities. If anyone could get a tip on the hundreds, the local crew trying to keep their pledge to the off-limits zone might. Then again, they could be playing me. I cruised past a dusty playground. The concrete basketball court was empty and unlined, the iron rims bent like the tongues of tired dogs.

I thought of the street games I'd found soon after I'd moved out of South Philly to the town house up near Jefferson Hospital. Down Tenth Street was a one-court park that held a competitive game on the weekend. I'd been playing there for a month, getting into more and more games when the regulars figured out I was willing and able to play defense and could pull a rough rebound as well as anyone on the court. I was often the only white guy there and they started calling me Bobby Jones after the 76ers defensive star.

One Saturday a group of challengers rolled in swaggering. One called game before he was even past the fence and everyone started posturing and trash talking and making their side bets.

When it came time to pick up, the local guy who had next let me sit until his final choice and then made his play: "We take the old white guy make it easy on your ass an' you buck up the bet another Jackson." The new man looked at me, snorted and peeled off another twenty-dollar bill.

I had learned over the years that as the minority on the ball courts the best tactic was to stay obscure, keep your mouth shut, and do the quiet things that win games and keep you playing. The real players are not dumb. They like to win. They'll pick you to play for their own purposes, regardless of color.

We won by six and I had only one basket but more assists and rebounds than anyone else on the court. After the game the local guy winked at me but never said a word. He collected his cash and I assume split it with his boys later. I picked up my ball and went home to get ready for a night shift.

I'd lost my bearings on my trip to the past and looked up at the street sign to realize I was driving east. It was late afternoon, the temperature had crawled up near eighty and I decided to stop in at Kim's. Maybe I was hoping to run into McCane, find an excuse. But the bar was nearly empty. The same young bartender had an old Don Henley tune turned up on the jukebox and I sat in McCane's seat. She brought me an ale.

"Good memory," I said, putting cash on the bar.

"You and the good 'ol boy from Moultrie," she said. "Where is your buddy, anyway? He don't usually miss the TNT movie. Likes all those old ones, you know, like *High Plains Drifter* and *Catch-22* and stuff."

I noticed the sound on the corner television was muted. Henley was singing about all the things he thought he'd figured out that he'd have to learn again. She had the air conditioning turned up high and the lights already low.

"Did you say Moultrie?" I asked. "I thought he was from Charleston?"

"Might have been. But he sure knows about the state pen near Moultrie," she said, working the glassware under the bar even though there wasn't a soul drinking but me.

"Said he was a bull there and I should know. My daddy did some time there when I was a kid."

I wondered why McCane had skipped this part of his résumé, not that we were on reminiscing terms.

"Must have been before I met him," I said.

She poured another beer from the tap and took my empty. I watched the lights playing in the bar's back mirrors through my second and left her a five-dollar tip on the way out the door. When I got to the truck I called Billy.

"Did you ever do a full dossier on McCane?" I asked, and it must have been in my voice. Billy was usually steps ahead of me and I had a feeling it got to his pride when he wasn't.

"No. I just verified that he works for the insurance company. Why? You find out he belongs to the Klan or something?"

Billy is not usually a vindictive person.

"We need to track his work background," I said. "He told me he had been a cop in Charleston and Savannah, but we need to find out if he ever had any connection with the state pen near Moultrie."

Billy was quiet on the other end, spinning the information in his head, frustrated by the lack of logic.

"You want to connect the dots on this one for me?" he finally said.

"It might be nothing," I said. "But let's check."

Old cop thinking. Someone lies to you, there's a reason, even if it's a lie by omission. Maybe McCane just didn't include it because being a prison guard isn't exactly a revered position in law enforcement. Maybe there was more. Maybe I was paranoid. I drove north up the oceanside highway, watching the surf work at the Florida sand. Maybe I was back in the game.

20

When I got to Billy's apartment, he was still in his back office, working the computers. I opened a beer and watched over his shoulder while he ran his fingers over the keyboard, popping up government websites and directories. He'd run McCane's dossier and there were some major gaps in it, and that often meant that the person you were trying to track had either spent time in the system, or was in law enforcement, or had somehow had his history expunged. Billy had then called a prosecutor friend in Atlanta who lowered his voice when Billy asked him if Frank McCane's name and the prison at Moultrie rang any bells. He asked Billy not to use him as a source, but told him the story.

"McCane was a d-dayshift guard at the prison and had b-been there for several years. After a change in the governor's seat, there was a c-crackdown on the Department of Correction's internal system, which had been rife with abuse," Billy said. "McCane had b-been the unofficial head of a shakedown club among the guards."

"So he was indicted?"

"Not exactly." Billy said. "When they backed him into a corner with proof, he made a d-deal with the governor's office, t-turned over information on the warden and gave up his job. The only s-stipulation was lifelong p-probation. He could no longer w-work for the state, and if he was ever arrested on the outside, they'd re-file the whole l-load of charges from the p-prison on him."

"So he moved out of the state, gave up public police work and went with the insurance job," I said, putting the obvious into the air. "Your friend give any details on what McCane specialized in during this stellar career?"

"Very little," Billy said. "He's a state p-prosecutor. It's a political year in Georgia. N-No one's going to b-be in the mood to hang their butt out."

I drained the beer and went for another. Billy declined to join me and I changed my own mind on my way to the refrigerator. The Moultrie prison was stuck in my head from a Philadelphia case, and I was trying to dig it out of its place in the past. I started a pot of coffee.

"Can you find a *Philadelphia Inquirer* archive on the box?" I called back to him while the coffee was brewing.

"Sure. What are we looking for?"

"Name of an inmate. A guy we tried to help out after we broke a car theft ring. The bust went bad and a port officer got killed. This guy was a locksmith at the time and he ended up on the rotten end of a murder charge."

"They would have done a news story at the time?"

"I hope so."

While Billy clicked at the computers, I sat at the kitchen counter telling him the story, unraveling a day at a Delaware River port warehouse in a time before I was a completely disillusioned police detective.

A handful of us had been assigned to an auto theft task force that was working with Customs on the theft and importation of cars and trucks from the northeast to Haiti and the Caribbean.

The feds had been working the scam up and down the coast. The theft ring was the typical game. At the low end, they hired car thieves to do the heists. The boosters were given special lists of makes and models, actual orders to fill. Most of the cars were high-end SUVs, especially Toyota 4Runners. At the time, the loose pack of military thugs running Haiti had a liking for the all-terrain vehicles. The Toyota emblem on the front of the hood looked distinctly like a bull with horns, and to them the bull image carried an aura of masculine power. The SUVs brought top dollar.

The car thieves were told the less damage the more they would get paid, and they'd boost the cars and park them in a commuter lot at Philly International Airport to be sure they didn't have anti-theft locators. If the cops traced the electronic beacon, all they'd get was the car abandoned at the airport.

Once the cars cooled, the shippers would then move them inside a warehouse at the port where a guy could cut a key. When they were ready, a tractor-trailer would back up to the warehouse loading dock and the cars would be driven inside. The crew would then pack the rest of the trailer, floor to ceiling, with household goods, boxes of clothes, bags of rice. If an inspector decided to pop the back door, all he could see in the first ten feet were legitimate goods for shipping.

"What do you think? Five years ago?" Billy said from the other room, still clicking.

"No, more like seven."

Most of the task force work had been with informants, kids picked up on auto theft charges who were looking to deal information for a break. We'd put surveillance on a warehouse and it was primed. I was one of four detectives, a U.S. Customs agent, and a handful of port police used to cut off any escape routes. We were in position. It was hot and dusty as we leaned into a corrugated wall around the corner.

"Summertime," I said to Billy.

"I think I've got it," he said.

We waited in the heat until the tractor-trailer was loaded and started to pull away on its route to the holding area, where the container would be loaded onto an outbound freighter to Haiti. When the trailer cleared the doors we jumped, guns drawn.

"U.S. Customs, hands in the air!" the agent yelled as three of us came through the front and two more took down a door to the back.

The element of surprise. Four men were eating lunch around a wire-spool table, another was in the glass-walled office, sleeping with his feet on the desktop. One was busy near the back of the warehouse, his head down and a pair of safety glasses on his face while he worked over a machine. He was my guy—the key man.

It would have gone down like clockwork but for the idiot in the john. The last one to see us had to be the cowboy.

Everyone in the warehouse had already let the air out of their lungs when the asshole came sprinting out of the cheap wooden door of the bathroom and started firing a second-rate .38, thinking he might get to the loading dock door. He made it twenty feet before he took four rounds and dropped. But one of his random shots also hit a port policeman.

"Harlan P. Moticker," Billy said from his room. "The locksmith."

"That's him," I said, walking into the study.

Harlan was the outsider in the group, hired to cut the keys for the stolen vehicles so they could go abroad in no-fuss driving condition. He was a southern boy down on his luck, trying to make a go of it up north and making extra cash on the wrong side.

All seven men were arrested and when the port cop died of his wound, the ante got raised. Because a person had died during the commission of a felony, they were all charged with murder.

"Can you check the Department of Corrections in Georgia to see if he's still in?"

Billy had already pushed his chair to the other screen.

Harlan P. was the only one of the group who wasn't connected to the offshore ring. As a result, he was the only one who had nothing to deal. He had no useful information for Customs, so no matter how much he wanted to cooperate he still ate the whole twenty-five to life. He'd been paid two hundred dollars for the job.

"Harlan P. Moticker, prisoner ID #3568649. The Haverford State Correctional Facility in Moultrie," Billy read.

I suppose I'd felt for the guy. When we were writing up the case the older guys in the squad kept forwarding the calls from his young wife to me. He pleaded guilty to avoid a trial and when his attorney asked to have him swapped to a Georgia prison near his family for a Philadelphia mob flunky who wanted to come home, I was the one who gave the department's blessing. Nobody else cared.

Now I suppose I felt lucky.

By noon the next day I was driving a rental down a secondary highway in south Georgia. Billy had found me an early flight out of West Palm Beach and he'd also made a call to his prosecutor friend in Atlanta. The lawyer balked at first, but because he owed Billy, he made the request for a visit.

The warden at Haverford said he could not figure why a private investigator from Florida would want to talk with Moticker. The inmate was one of the better behaved and more trustworthy of his 612 convicts. But in the spirit of cooperation, he didn't object.

Well out of the city, the road I was on split an open forest of scrub pines and occasional patches of hardwood, and there were leaves on the forest floor. Here it was true fall. Colors not natural to South Florida dripped and fluttered in orange and red in the trees. Both the temperature and the humidity were under sixty. I rolled the windows down and inhaled the odor of sun-dried clay and slow-rotting leaves. It was almost idyllic—until I saw the flat sign for the prison and turned off onto a slowly curving blacktop road.

There were no buildings visible from the highway. It was just a well-maintained country road until I hit the guard gate to the parking area. I gave the man my name and while he checked I watched the sun glitter off a high, razor-wired fence in the distance. I had been inside prisons before and never liked the feeling.

The guard handed me a pass and pointed the way to administration. I parked, and as I followed the sidewalk I could see down the fence line to a guard tower where the silhouette of a marksman showed in the open window. Inside the offices I stood in a waiting area with uncomfortable cushioned chairs and a portrait of the new governor.

The warden's name was Emanuel T. Bowe and he greeted me with a firm handshake across a state-issue desk. He was a tall black man with gray hair cut in a flat top and a beard that was carefully trimmed to follow the edges of his jaw line. He looked more like a college professor than a southern prison warden.

"So, Mr. Freeman. You were a detective in Philadelphia when our Mr. Moticker was convicted, do I have that right?"

"Yes sir."

"And you are now working as a private detective on a case in South Florida?"

"Yes, sir. It's in the very preliminary stages, sir," I said, the lying coming easily since it was marginal.

"Well, I will be up-front with you, Mr. Freeman. I asked Mr. Moticker if he had any objections to speaking with you and although he said he remembered you and was willing, he seemed, as I am, perplexed as to what information he might have to help you."

I only nodded.

"Frankly, I have only been the warden here for eighteen months, but Mr. Moticker has been here quite some time and has earned a certain respect from both sides out there on the pound. I would not like to see anything change that."

"And neither would I, sir. I'm not sure he can help, but if he's willing, I'd like to give it a try," I said, giving nothing up, and hoping it was enough.

The warden stood up.

"Let's go, then."

An open walkway led out to the first gate, chain-link, with a guard dressed in brown with a radio clipped to his belt. No gun. No nightstick.

He greeted the warden, looked at me, and the first snap of dry metal let us through to a cinder-block control room. Inside a fishbowl of two-inch shatterproof glass another guard said hello to Bowe, and I was quickly run over with a security wand and had to hand over my keys. When we were ready, the guard hit the electronic lock on the second metal door and we were back outside.

"Warden on the pound," a loudspeaker announced.

The compound was a low-slung collection of dull yellow buildings with wide grassy areas between. Spokes of sidewalks led from one to the other. No bushes, trees or other vegetation. Nowhere to hide. There were a few men moving about, obviously inmates because they were dressed in faded blue instead of the guard's brown. They were not being escorted. One might think of a poor man's college campus until you lifted your eyes to the towers and the sight of long-barreled rifles reminded you.

"We're headed to the machine shop," Bowe said, moving swiftly, but not hurrying. "Mr. Moticker has been the senior mechanic for some time."

The warden's long legs made it difficult to keep up without looking like you were trying.

"One never runs across the pound," he said over his shoulder. "The sharpshooters are trained to sight in on anyone running and the guards are taught to run toward the towers if they are in danger so the shooters can take out any assailants."

I knew the philosophy, but the feeling of gunsights on my neck still made the muscles in my back tingle.

"Besides, it makes the inmates uneasy to have to wonder where you are running to and for what reason," he said with a smile that did not indicate anything funny. "Information is a valued thing inside."

It sounded like a warning, and I took it as such.

The machine shop was made up of three open bays and part of a second floor with glass-fronted classrooms. There was a yellow fire engine parked in the far bay and a handful of men were clustered around a rear bumper intently watching an inmate with a welding torch.

The guard who came to meet us was in a brown uniform but his sleeves were rolled up and there were black grease marks on his forearms and hands. He and Bowe spoke for a minute, too low for me to hear. The guard nodded and walked back toward the group.

"Thirty minutes is all I can give you, Mr. Freeman," Bowe said. "There's an inmate count at two o'clock and we keep a very tight schedule. I will collect you when you're through."

I thanked him and watched the guard tap the man with the torch on the shoulder. The inmate raised his face shield and turned to look our way. He handed his tools to another inmate, gave some instruction, and walked across the shop. He was a thin, jangly man. The points of his joints stuck out at his shoulders, elbows and knees. When he got close I could see the gray in his hair and a jagged white scar that crawled through one eyebrow and then over the bridge of his nose. I knew that he was thirty-seven years old. He looked fifty.

"Warden, sir," Moticker said, addressing the superintendent first and then turning to me. "Mr. Freeman, sir." We shook hands and his grip seemed purposely weak.

"Can we do this outside, sir?" Moticker said to the guard, who nodded his head. Only then did the inmate lead me out to a concrete slab just outside the raised, garage-style door. We sat on our heels in the sun but also in full view of the bay.

"How you doin', Harlan," I started.

"I'm okay, sir," he said, taking a single cigarette from his shirt pocket and lighting it with an old-style book of cardboard matches. He took a drag and cut his eyes into the bay.

"How's the family?"

"I see my son on occasion. He's got hisself close to graduatin'," he answered, letting the smoke out slowly. "My wife, well, we got divorced a few years back."

"I'm sorry," I said.

"I never did get to thank you for helpin' with the transfer, though," he said, looking me in the eye for the first time.

We were both silent, having run out of manners.

"I'll just get to it," I finally said. "I'm not a cop anymore, but I'm working a case out of Florida that has to do with an insurance investigator named Frank McCane."

I watched his eyes jump to mine without a movement of his head.

"I know he was a bull here for some time and your years overlapped some before he was, uh, dismissed. I was hoping you might tell me something about him."

"Ol' Milo," he said, a grin coming to his face. "An insurance man, you say? Ain't that a hoot."

Moticker took another slow drag and smiled with a set of bad teeth.

"You're familiar?"

"Oh, anybody who was around then is familiar with Milo," he said, lowering his already soft voice. "Mean sombitch and king of the pound, too. But that's a sore subject round here now, Mr. Freeman."

"I can appreciate that. But the record isn't too clear on his dismissal," I said. "I need a sense of the man without going to someone who might have been a friend or might get back to him."

This time Moticker's pale eyes stayed on mine, the eyes of a man with nothing to lose, but also one who rarely came across the opportunity to gain anything close to payback.

"McCane ran every damn thing in here at one time," he started. "He had a piece of the inside drug trade. He decided whose homemade buck got confiscated an' whose got sold. He controlled the inventory coming in and out of concession.

"Anybody had money, he squeezed 'em. Anybody had anything, he dealt it. Didn't matter what color or what kind. Pure mean and pure greedy, Mr. Freeman, that's the sense of that man."

Moticker finished the cigarette, carefully snubbed it out and put the butt in his pocket. He cut his eyes to the shop again.

"Milo was running the drug trade. Had other guards bringing the stuff in and then flushing the packages down the toilets before they came on the pound," he started, barely whispering.

"He knew the pump station. Would plug the thing by flushing an inmate shirt at the same time. Then he'd order one of the cons down into the station to clear it. Guy would go through the shit while the shooters and assistant warden just watched him get down in there and he would stuff the drug packages in his pockets and then come up with the shirt.

"Hell, nobody was gonna frisk that boy all covered with stink, and he'd get sent to the showers and later pass the dope off to Milo for a cut."

He refocused his eyes on the group of welders inside and seemed to reshelve the memory. "He was the kind of man who knew how to use people and still make them feel inferior," he finally said.

"The kind of man who might be involved with murder for money?" I asked.

The inmate seemed to roll his answer around in his mouth for a while.

"Not by hisself," he said. "Milo wouldn't be that dumb."

Moticker stood up and for the first time I could see a con's deviousness in his face.

"They'd be hell to pay if that ol' boy came back here as an inmate," he said, a crooked grin playing at his lips. "Hell to pay."

I could tell the possibility left him with a vision that could keep him warmly amused for a lot of boring nights on his bunk.

"One thing," I said. "Why Milo?"

He looked quizzically at me.

"The nickname?"

"Oh, hell, that was his own," he said. "Character out that old war movie *Catch-22*. Milo Minderbinder was the guy that was doin' all the underhanded dealin' getting' hisself rich off the war. McCane loved that."

We went back inside the shop and I shook his hand.

"Hope things work out," he said, and I wished him the same.

21

I sat on the hood of my truck, waiting for twilight, second-guessing my trust, and shooting holes in my own plans.

I'd ground out the possibilities during the flight back from Georgia and wasn't sure I hadn't wasted a bunch of time and Billy's money just to satisfy my need for logic. As the plane had lined up its approach several miles to the west of the West Palm airport I'd stared out on the unbroken sawgrass of the Everglades. Acres and acres of still untouched land glowing gold in the low sunlight. I missed my river. I wondered why I was not back on it, paddling, listening to it.

I had used the river to try to bury the memory of two bullets fired during a stickup on Thirteenth Street in Center City, Philadelphia. The round fired by a sixteen-year-old punk on the sidewalk had caught me in the neck, boring through muscle on its way through. The second round, mine, dropped a twelve-year-old accomplice as he bolted out the door behind his friend. The sidewalk vision of his small face and skinny, quiet chest had gouged my dreams ever since. Out of the hospital, I'd taken a disability buyout and moved from the city streets where I'd grown up the son of a cop. I wanted out and I wanted different. I'd sworn off the cops, but today I was back out in the northwest section of the city, watching the light leak out of the alley and then the trees. I'd turned another corner and wasn't sure why.

When the strings of cloud in the west turned a burnt orange on their edges and the sky went to a cobalt blue, I climbed into the truck and drove toward the dope hole.

I knew from my time on the beat how much the landscape and rhythm and people of a place change when the light seeps away. When I patrolled the downtown areas of Center City on the graveyard shift I would get up in the daytime and patronize the same delis and music shops along Thirteenth and Arch when the real people dominated the sidewalks instead of the hustlers and bums of the night. More than a few times I questioned which world I felt more comfortable in.

I turned at a light with a hanging street sign labeled Thirty-first Avenue in large letters and M.L. King Boulevard in smaller script below. On either side of the road were one- and two-story apartments, arranged like old cheap motels with long, grassless courtyards down the middle and the doors and single windows facing in. They had been painted a bilious green and you could tell from the texture of the paint that there were uncounted layers underneath. Down the street a sign stood in front of an identical block of buildings that read, FOR RENT. HOUSING AUTHORITY. SECTION 8 UNITS AVAILABLE. INQUIRE AT HOUSING OFFICE.

The physical structure was different, but it was just another version of the Washington Street projects in Philly, where I once answered a sick-baby call and had dishes and a brick tossed onto my patrol car from some apartment above.

I turned at another intersection onto the seller's avenue. There was movement along the sidewalks: people, women and older men, who seemed to have places to go. But there was also a nervousness gathering in the air, an anticipation among the younger men waiting for the early evening trade to begin. I found a spot on the east side of the road in the shadow of a big oak about a block from the action.

In a few minutes I could pick out the players. The sullen guy with his head down and eyes up had spotted me right off. But he was cool. The long black pants with the ironed crease set him aside from the young ones who were no doubt his runners. The dope would never be on any of them for more than a few seconds and only during the exchange for money through an open car window. The stash would be back in some hidey-hole in the alley or under some fender of an innocent man's bumper. The customers would pull up—some white, some black—and slow or stop in front of the man, looking for a signal which was not going to come as long as I was parked down the street. Some were bold enough, or desperate enough, to roll down their passenger windows and call out to the dealer. He ignored them, turning his head away in my direction and saying nothing.

After forty-five minutes I watched a woman of indeterminate age come up the sidewalk, hips swinging unsteadily. She was dressed in a wrinkled summer skirt and a short top that showed her bare midriff, ribs poking out from the bottom. She stumbled once on her blocky high heels. She was trying to look like an unconcerned girl on a stroll. But her path was deliberate.

When she got to the dealer she stopped, two arm lengths away, and put a hand on her hip. He looked the other way. I could see her head bobbing as she talked, each shift of her hip putting her another step closer. Suddenly, in a movement like a snake strike, the man's hand flicked out and caught her flush across the face. The violence of it made my own hand jump to the door handle, but I sat still. The girl stumbled back. None of the runners reacted. They kept their eyes to the street as if the bitch-slap was either expected, or a regular occurrence.

The woman slunk away and the man resettled himself on a tall wooden stool. He pulled straight the crease in his trousers and then looked up in my direction as if daring me to make a move. I couldn't have done a thing. I wasn't wearing a badge and had to take a grain of solace that I was killing his business for a couple of hours.

22

Momma never said a word. Now Eddie was invisible to her, too.

He'd sat in the house too long. The drugs were long since gone. He was hungry, both for food and another high. He still had some of Mr. Harold's money in his pocket. The light was dying through the living room window, so he went out. Under a few bags of bottles and some chunks of aluminum window framing, he found his old winter coat in his cart. He knew it wasn't winter. He would know when the city started putting up the Kwanzaa banners on Sistrunk Boulevard that winter was coming. But he put the coat on today because he was still shivering.

Eddie had made a decision in the silence of his momma's house. He would go back to the liquor store and wait for Mr. Harold to show up. It was either there or the jail where he'd first met him. But he didn't want to go near the jail. Mr. Harold had told him to never come to the jail or the money would stop. And Mr.

Harold had been the only one in the forensics ward who really sat and listened to Eddie. The liquor store. It was the only place he had. But first he'd need a bundle to get through.

When he got to Thirteenth and Court he stopped at the corner like he always did to watch the place. He pretended to look in the Dumpster at Ringold's but that's not where his eyes went. There was something different on the street and he could smell it. Eddie knew his days and this should be a busy one. But the runners weren't moving and the street was cold. Eddie pulled his coat tighter.

There was only one potential buyer, in a blue pickup parked near the big oak tree, but he couldn't see from here what color the man was who sat unmoving inside. Eddie pushed the cart forward and saw the girl coming up the sidewalk. He watched her walking hard, her blocky shoes scuffing. She was a junkie. Eddie had tried to lure her to go with him before but she always spat at him and told him to keep his nigger ass away.

That was all right. Eddie just quietly made the offer. If they accepted, he would give them what they wanted and then get what he wanted. That's the way it worked.

As she got closer Eddie could hear her cussing and could see the wetness leaking through the hand she held to her face. He moved on, distracted but hungry. When he got close to the Brown Man's runners he could feel them step away instead of moving closer to the man as usual. Eddie pushed his cart closer. One of the runners spit out a harsh whisper, "What you doin', junk man? Cain't you see five-oh on the street?"

Eddie never raised his head, never turned around. He just bent over to pick up a beer can and cut his eyes back to the blue pickup that he'd forgotten after the girl. Police on the street?

The white man in the driver's seat looked directly at him. Not past him at the Brown Man. Not through him like everyone else did. He was looking Eddie straight in the face in a way that no person had done in years on the street, and it scared him.

It was then that the marked patrol car came around the corner and Eddie heard the Brown Man say "Fuck" in a low growl. Eddie stood up and pushed away, feeling the cold eyes of the man in the truck on him like two icy nickels being pressed against the skin on the back of his neck.

I sat watching the dealer on his stool, his wooden throne on the street. The sneer and quick pop of anger had blown a hole in his act of nonchalance. He didn't like me messing with his action, but he also knew he'd be here tomorrow, and the next day. He knew his customers wouldn't go away like I would. I'd done my stints on the narcotics cases and done the proselytizing to the local kids when I was walking a beat. I'd stroll up into a group off South Street and know from the active hands going to pockets what was up. I'd try to be cool, say what's up fellas. They would avoid eye contact except for the one ballsy one who would look me in the face and sarcastically call me officer.

To him I'd give the speech about the penalty for possession with intent to sell, the mandatory minimums. And as often as not he'd recite the correct amounts of product needed to constitute a charge of intent. The others would hide whatever grin was crawling onto their faces. They were smart enough not to push it. Ballsy guy was not. So I would position my body and cut him off from the others, back him to a wall like a good fighter cutting off the ring and without touching him I'd get my face close and watch his eyes widen like a bad fighter knowing he's in trouble. The eyebrows would raise and he'd say "What?" By then I would have tilted up my nightstick from its metal ring on my belt and would have stuck the rounded end up into the vulnerable notch where ribs meet below the sternum and I would push.

"Not on my beat," I would say, only loud enough for him to hear. "Not on my street."

If he nodded, I would let them walk away and I would stand and watch them. Sometimes they would go in silence. Sometimes from a block away I would hear one yell, "Fuck you, cop." Either way I would wonder why I was out there.

I was thinking the same thing today when I picked up the dark figure in the corner of my eye.

He was a big man, shrouded in a long dark coat in seventy-degree weather. He was pushing a grocery cart down the sidewalk in a slow, lethargic pace. His head was tucked down into his thick shoulders like a big, wary tortoise, and he seemed to be mumbling to himself. Then as I watched, he deftly, too deftly, steered the cart effortlessly around a milk crate in his path and then through the drug runners. I was trying to place him, recall where I'd seen his shape before when he bent to pick up a can. I watched the hand slide out of the coat cuffs and swallow the can and that's when he looked up and I saw his eyes. They were black hollows, set deep in a face that was dark and emotionless. I could not blink and suddenly felt a fine ripple of muscle along my spine like a traveling drop of sweat.

The yelp of a siren snapped my head away. Blue lights flashed three times in my rearview, and in my side mirror I saw the cop opening the door of his patrol car.

"Stay in the vehicle," he said over his P.A. system. He got out of his car and stood for a moment. And then I watched him walk up, hand on the butt of his holstered gun. I checked my other side mirror and saw his partner standing behind his opened door, looking through my back window. Two-man patrol, I thought, a luxury in Philly.

When I looked back up the street, the big junk man was gone. It had only been seconds, but he had disappeared. Two residents were poking their heads out of partially opened doors.

"That's a good place for your hands, sir," the approaching cop said, staying close to the body of the truck and back over my left shoulder. I had already put my hands up on top of the steering wheel, knowing what made these guys nervous.

"License and registration, please."

For some inane reason, maybe it was just biological to the species, I said, "Is there a problem, officer?"

He took the paperwork without a word. He was a young guy, mid-twenties, wearing a hard and uncomfortable bulletproof vest under his uniform shirt.

"You're the wrong color in the wrong place at the wrong time, Mr., uh, Freeman."

I turned my head to look more fully at him and he seemed older and dumber all at once. He said something behind the cab to his partner and then into the microphone clipped to his shoulder lapel, "Sixteen, Echo One."

"Echo One," came the response. The voice sounded familiar.

"We got a stop here off Twenty-seventh on the drug run that fits your BOLO on suspicious persons."

"Echo One responding."

The cop again said something to his partner and then began writing off my license.

"White man in the wrong place," I said, unable to keep my mouth shut. "That's a real specific BOLO, officer."

The cop stopped writing, but didn't look up.

"Freeman," he said. "Is that Jewish?"

The question was spoken, but mouthed into the air, like he was just pondering the possibility. I tightened my mouth. This time I did keep it shut, and waited for Richards to arrive.

When a dark SUV finally pulled up, I popped the handle to get out but the movement rattled the patrol cop. He was back leaning on the open door of his cruiser and fumbled his pad and reached for his holster.

"Calm down, son," I said, raising my palms. "I know these people."

"Hey, hey. *Tranquilo* Taylor," said the Cuban detective climbing out of the SUV's driver side.

"This man is the infamous Max Freeman," he said with a flourish. "Both a friend to and a pain in the ass of all law enforcement."

Detective Vincente Diaz came around the truck with his junior executive smile in place and his hand extended.

"Max, Max, Max. Long time, amigo. Sherry said she had seen you and here you are, in the flesh and hip deep in the middle of another of your investigations."

He shook my hand vigorously and as usual I couldn't tell if he was being sarcastic or friendly.

Diaz had partnered up with Richards when she came into the detective bureau. The wiry strength in his small hands offset the pleasant, white-toothed smile.

"Hey, Max. What, fishing is no good out in the jungle? You got to come slumming in our pond?"

"I know you better, Vince," I said. "Your partner tells you everything."

He looked at me with that playful raised eyebrow.

"No, no, no. Not everything, eh?"

Richards was coming around the SUV, looking at the patrol officer.

"We got this, Taylor," she said.

"Yeah, well, I still got to take a photo for the field in-

vestigation file," he said, showing the old Polaroid he
kept in the backseat.

"Believe me, Taylor," she said. "Neither your L.T.
nor Chief Hammonds want to see this guy's name on
an F.I. card."

The cop shrugged and facetiously muttered, "Yes,
ma'am," and got back into his car, put it in gear and
backed away.

"Max," Richards said, finally acknowledging me.

"Detective."

"You got something for us, or is this just a coincidence?"

"I do have some bait out. No bites yet," I said.

"Couldn't have been out there long."

"Actually, I wasn't sure where the current might
take it."

"But this lovely area is a possibility?"

"Always."

Diaz was watching us, like a fan at a bad tennis
match.

"You two going to go on like this for a while? Cause
I'll go roust some Dumpster divers or something else
more productive if you want?"

Richards smiled.

While all three of us leaned against the box of my
truck, Richards told me the sheriff's office had moved
to step up their presence and visibility in the zone. Although detectives were rarely called to the street without a specific crime, the honchos had sent down word
to have certain suspicious situations checked out.

"Like . . ."

"A white guy in a fancy truck sitting alone watching the busiest dope corner in the county," Diaz finished my response.

"I got to think you're off on this theory of yours, Freeman," he continued. "Our guy doing the rapes has to be some low-life just shagging girls when he can. He's got to be some zone cat and if these people would just wise up and help us out with some information, we'd have his ass sitting on Old Sparky up at Raiford."

He made sure his voice was loud enough for the handful of residents still on their front steps to hear. Two more cars started turning down the street but quickly straightened their wheels and rolled away.

"My esteemed partner believes your theory about a local acting as a hit man for the insurance companies is marginal," Richards said.

"How is some moke from in here going to hook up with that kind of scam anyway?" Diaz broke in again. "These are not your rocket scientists of crime out here. Even if your motive is right, Freeman, the two cases are in no way linked. Your guy is too smart. Maybe out-of-town work. Carlyle there would call up and spill on anybody who was out here fuckin' with his territory by bringing in more scrutiny by us," he said, pointing to the empty stool the dealer had abandoned.

"Carlyle?"

"Yeah," Diaz grinned. "The dealer. His momma probably named him so he'd grow up tough. Instead he grows up and takes on the illustrious street name

Brown Man and makes it as a drug peddler just to get her back."

"You ever have a conversation with Carlyle?" I said.

"One-sided," Diaz said.

"So he's not real forthcoming with information?"

"But he'd still give up some cheap local out snuffing old ladies just to keep his trade moving."

"And nobody's got a C.I. who's close to him?"

Diaz looked around again. Some of the neighbors had wandered back into their homes, some had pulled out lawn chairs as if an early evening show was only minutes away.

"What can I say, amigo? You see these people out when the drug shop is open? No. They're afraid," he said. "Carlyle got his territory set, for now. And believe me, the last thing he wants is local trouble."

As we talked I kept cutting my eyes to Richards, caught her watching. The sun was well down but the air was still warm.

"You two done tilting at windmills for now?" she said.

Diaz shook his head.

"Hard as nails and literate too, man," he said. "You ever have a partner like this, Max?"

Richards was silent, listening for my answer.

"Hey," I finally said. "Cervantes was Hispanic. What do I know?"

The radios on both of their belts ran a simultaneous string of static and then squawked, "Fourteen, Echo One."

Diaz snatched the call, lowered the volume and walked around to the front of the truck. Richards and I stood in a quiet that seemed oddly uncomfortable.

"The skeptic," she finally said. "He only wishes he didn't care."

I grinned and looked at her. Even in the dark her eyes were showing color.

"You got something going?" she said.

"I got a long shot out," I said.

"No. I mean tonight."

"Uh, no," I said. "I mean no, not really."

"Come by later?"

"Sure," I managed.

"I'll make some coffee," she said.

"Okay partner," Diaz interrupted. "We got to hit the road."

Richards turned away and started toward the SUV and Diaz shook my hand.

"I hate to say it, Freeman, but I'll see you," he said with a grin. "Be careful, man."

Eddie slipped between two buildings and into the alley, running from the cold spot on the back of his neck.

He rounded the corner of Twenty-seventh Avenue and pushed the cart east, the loose wheel spinning maniacally, his shadow cast out in front from the last light pole. Who was the white man in the truck? And how could he see him?

Eddie liked routine, and his routine was going to hell. Mr. Harold didn't show. He couldn't get his dope. Momma wasn't talking and now a white man's eyes had looked into him and Eddie was wondering if his invisibility was also gone.

He shrugged up into his coat. A car rolled past, the bass from its stereo rippling through him. He pushed on to Second Street and then cruised the back alley of the row, stopping at Louise's Kitchen where he found a plastic bag of bread heels hung up on a hook above the Dumpster. Louise put it out there because she knew the bums would root through her garbage if she didn't make it easy for them. So she hung the bread up away from the rats. Eddie knew when the bag came out and he was surprised to see it still there. He sat on the bottom of the steps leading up into the back of the restaurant, chewing through several pieces of the bread. The smell of the alley did not register. His own odor, rising up from his collar all warm and ripe from the body heat trapped under his coat did not register. Mr. Harold, Eddie thought, an idea pulling at him.

23

When Eddie crossed over the railroad tracks, he had officially crossed over to the east side, and he knew enough to be careful on the east side. By now it was dark, but the street lamps and still-lighted windows in the business buildings pushed Eddie to the shadows. When he made his way to a spot under the Intracoastal bridge he sat there for an hour, tucked back against cold concrete. He wished he'd gotten the heroin before he tried this. He was feeling the need in his stomach. Just a single pop would do.

The smell of the river was a blend of salt and gasoline fumes and damp pilings. Above he could hear the roll of cars on the bridge surface, humming along the concrete and then singing when the tires hit the metal grating in the middle. He checked the time on the watch from deep in his pocket, left the cart and started over to the parking lot of the county jail.

He stayed close to the fence, moving from tree to

tree. The eastsiders thought landscaping made things look nice, so there was always a dark shadow to slip into. He scanned the lot. Most of the light glowed up off the eight-story white stone façade of the jail. But Eddie could still make out the colors and makes of the cars. The fourth row down and in between the two light poles was Mr. Harold's Caprice.

He knew that the doctor worked the middle shift and would be getting off at 11:00 P.M., plenty of time.

He found a way through the fencing, a gap left open by workers at an adjoining construction site, and moved low and slow along an inside row to the car. He peered up over the line of hoods and watched a single, twirling yellow light moving along the front sidewalk. That was the thing about those security carts, you always knew where they were.

When it disappeared, Eddie moved to the driver's-side door of the Caprice and reached into his pocket for the old tennis ball he'd brought from his cart. He turned the ball in his fingers to find the shaved side and located the small hole that he'd punched into its middle with a nail. Then he positioned the hole over the round key entrance on the door lock. Holding the seal tight with one hand, he took one more wary look around, then banged the ball with the heel of his other hand. The air from the ball rushed into the lock system hard enough to simultaneously pop up all four of the door buttons. Eddie opened the left passenger door and climbed in.

The inside smelled of cigarettes and paper. A box of files sat in the back but there was still room for Eddie behind the driver's seat. He flipped the overhead light off, locked the doors and waited, his nose twitching with the smell of stale nicotine.

Eddie was in the backseat less than an hour when he heard footsteps on the pavement. Mr. Harold fumbled with his keys and then unlocked the doors. He tossed a briefcase onto the front passenger side and was already halfway in when the smell caused his face to screw up and he felt a huge hand clamp onto his upper right arm and pull him in.

The doctor whimpered once before his eyes snapped around to Eddie's and then quickly changed from wide-open shock to a narrow questioning.

"Jesus, Eddie. What the hell are you doing here?" said Harold Marshack, his voice jumping from surprise to consternation. "Didn't I tell you not to come here?"

Eddie stared at him and for the second time in only a few hours, another man's eyes looked back. The psychiatrist could see the edge of panic there.

"Hey, it's not safe for you here, Eddie," Marshack said, his voice now going calm and pitched as if he were speaking to a child.

"You didn't come to the post office," Eddie said.

His big hand was still holding the doctor's arm, a soft grip for Eddie, painful for the recipient. Marshack again changed his voice.

"I'll admit I wasn't sure what to do, Eddie," he said, now patting the big man's hand, hoping to ease the hold.

"A man was killed, Eddie. At Ms. Thompson's.

What happened, Eddie? Do you want to tell me what happened?"

Eddie knew the sound of those words. He'd heard that voice that said "Stupid Eddie" all his life. When he was a kid they lured him into the circle with the mock friendship just to steal his money or humiliate him for laughs. The women, the police, even Momma's preacher. Be nice to Eddie, then when his grip loosens, steal what he has. Eddie wasn't stupid.

"I do not know," he said to the doctor.

"Eddie, there's a problem," Marshack said, patting the big man's hand again. But the hand stayed.

"What? I did my job. I need my money," Eddie said. "I did what we said. I need what's mine."

The psychiatrist was quiet, thinking over the possibilities that might be running through his former patient's head.

"The woman's not dead, Eddie. She's still here. The old man's gone but Ms. Thompson is still alive. The police came, Eddie. She isn't dead."

Eddie's first reaction was to think "liar." They always lied to him. But his second reaction was to replay the night in his head. The pillow on Ms. Thompson's face. The old man coming out of the bathroom. Eddie's hand on his throat, feeling the bones fold. He'd made sure, damn sure, that the old guy was gone and then laid him out on the bed. Ms. Thompson did not move. She was gone, too. He was trying to see it in his head. No one could lay that still, that quiet, 'specially the old ladies.

He could feel the doctor's eyes on him.

"I do not know," he finally said. "But I need *my* money, Mr. Harold."

The doctor could feel the pressure on his arm. The big man's grip tightening with tension.

"OK, Eddie, sure. It was a mistake. We're still friends, right?" He worked his free hand into his jacket pocket and came out with his wallet. He opened the fold and riffled the bills inside with his thumb. In the dim light Eddie could see the corners of twenties flashing.

"Hundreds," Eddie said, his tone gone flat. "I got to have hundreds."

The big man's hand tightened again when he said it. His blunt fingertips had found the artery running under Marshack's biceps. They cut off the flow of blood, and the doctor was losing feeling down in his hand.

"Sure, Eddie. Sure. What was I thinking? In the glove box, the envelope, like always."

Marshack tried to move his arm, to reach for the passenger side. Eddie let his grip loose and the doctor reached over and twisted the lock.

24

I found Richards's house, rolled slowly past and pulled a U-turn at the intersection and parked across the street. It was a quiet neighborhood of small bungalow-style homes built back in the '40s in what was then a small southern town growing up at the mouth of a river to the ocean. The older houses were mostly wood clapboard with enclosed screen porches and they all sat up on short pilings to get them up off the moist ground. I could smell the oleander in the air and could make out the shapes of live oak canopies backlit by moonlight.

It was almost eleven. I'd been here before. I'd convinced her I was a restaurant idiot and taken her to dinner, her choice. We'd gone to movies she suggested. There was the one with the kid who sees ghosts. The ending had made her quiet afterward. Finally, while we were sitting in a coffee shop afterward, she asked if I believed in such things. "Everybody's got ghosts," I'd said. Brilliant, Freeman. When I'd dropped her off her good-bye caught in her throat.

A few weeks after I'd been late making it in from the river and we'd missed the start of a show she had tickets for. But she didn't seem to mind and we ended up sitting here on the back porch, talking about the past. The cop stuff was inevitable, but she avoided the subject of her husband and I stayed away from my family. Part of the wall was mine. Part was hers.

I rapped lightly on the screen door and waited. Nothing. I knocked a bit harder but it sounded like a hammer in the quiet. Through a window I could see soft light in a back room, so I stepped off the porch and found the wooden gate to the yard. I flipped the metal latch to make some noise and followed a path of flagstones. I could see the glow of aqua light before rounding the corner, and then her silhouette against the light of the pool. She was running an aluminum pole with a net on the end over the surface and was wearing shorts and a sleeveless T-shirt.

"A little late for maintenance," I said.

My voice made her jump, but only a little.

"I thought you'd stood me up, Freeman," she said, turning her head but keeping a grip on the pole. "Figured why waste a good wine buzz."

She made a final pass with the net, capturing a few more leaves that had dropped from the oak that dominated the yard, and then laid the pole aside.

"You're ahead of me," I said.

"I only offered coffee, Freeman. But I'll let you indulge."

She stepped up onto the wide, wood-planked porch and headed toward a set of French doors. When I started to follow she turned quickly and said, "I'll bring it out." I had still never been inside her house.

Her yard was thick with tropical plants, broad-leafed banana palms and white birds-of-paradise. The pool reflected up into some Spanish moss hanging from the closest oak limbs. Few of the plantings were native, but the effect was a soft, green, isolated place. The porch included a huge woven hammock stretched across one end.

In a few minutes she came out with a bottle and two wineglasses.

"Hey, it's not your wilderness," she said, reading my appreciation. "But it isn't bad for the city."

She filled the glasses and sat down on the top step, stretching her legs and putting the bottle next to her.

"Diaz doesn't think much of your theory, but he likes you," she said.

"Is that good?" I said, sitting down.

"Sure. It means he won't bring your name up to Hammonds for a while." She was looking into the pool.

"Hammonds approved the stepped-up patrol in the zone?"

"Yeah. But I'm not sure if he was shamed into it or if it was politics. The black city commissioner has been rattling the cages, and the newspapers are finally starting to run stories about 'A pattern of unsolved rapes and homicides in the minority community,' " she said with a pretty credible television news anchor's voice.

"I don't read the papers," I said.

"What? No delivery on the river?"

She was smiling and the space inside the circle it always created felt comfortable. I took another swallow of wine and leaned back, propped myself on my elbows and looked up through the oak. Night-blooming jasmine was on the air, mixed with a slightly sharp odor of chlorine.

"How's the leg wound?" she said, and I felt her hand on my thigh where a killer's bullet had caught me on a ricochet. She had been there when they found me bleeding in my shack.

"It'll hold up," I said, reaching up to curl a loose strand of her hair and letting the backs of my fingers brush her cheek.

She tilted her head into my hand and then leaned down and kissed me, the scent of wine and perfume spilling into my mouth and my breath catching in my chest.

The aqua glow caught just the edges of her hair and lit them. But her eyes were in shadow and I couldn't see their color.

25

An electronic warble pulled me out of a half sleep and Richards was up and out of the hammock before my eyes could clear. I just caught a slip of fabric and a flash of blonde hair going through the French doors as I lay there swinging, back and forth, with the force of her leaving.

It was still dark but there was a hint of dawn in the east. I could hear her voice, low and curt. Paged, I thought. A cop who is always on.

A light went on somewhere inside and a couple of minutes later she came out on the deck in a robe. Her hair was brushed and her eyelashes were wet from splashing water onto her face.

"They're calling detectives in on an overnight homicide," she said. "Some shrink who works in the jail was found with his throat cut."

Behind my eyes the dry sponge of a wine hangover was dulling both my eyesight and my brain synapses.

"He worked for you guys?"

"Not officially. We run the jail but the medical staff is contracted through a private company. But it doesn't look good having even a subcontractor get hit in your own jurisdiction."

I could see her head spinning the scene already. Motive and opportunity.

"Shit. We'll be chasing patients the guy's seen for years who are out on the street. They're going to want this one quick."

She came closer and put her hands on my shoulders and bent to kiss me. I was about to say something witty about duty calling when she twisted away.

"I gotta go. Call me," she said, moving to the doors and closing them behind her.

I spent the rest of the morning at Billy's. When I came through the lobby, Murray gave me a few more seconds of eye contact than usual and I thought I could see a slight grin playing at his mouth. I know it's just locker-room humor that people can tell, but how the hell would he know where I'd spent the night?

Billy had long since gone to his office and the apartment was immaculate. He had left a note on top of two large manila envelopes:

Max. This is the Thompson file, including a full dossier and confirmation that she did indeed have a viatical policy through a company other than McCane's and sold it to the same investment group as the others.

*The other file is a full dossier on Dr. Harold Mar-
shack, our possible middleman.
Let me know when you get in.*

I showered and changed and started a pot of coffee.
While I waited I started leafing through the Thompson
file. The woman had purchased an inordinately large
life insurance policy in 1954 and had been paying loy-
ally for decades. She obviously liked the idea of tuck-
ing such death insurance away so much that in the late
'70s, she bought yet another policy that gave her
nearly $100,000 in coverage. But four years ago she
sold both to the investment group for $40,000. They
had required a medical exam, but when they found
she had been diagnosed with cancer and had refused
surgery, they didn't hesitate.

Different figures, but pretty much the same pattern as the others. I poured myself a cup of coffee
and took the other file to the patio. Out on the ocean
there were a dozen fishing boats strung out past
what I knew was the third reef line. The water was
flat and a huge freighter was southbound on the
horizon, the visibility so clear I could see the lump of
a wave being pushed by the prow of the big vessel. I
sat in one of the patio chairs and opened the file on
Marshack.

The doctor, who was fifty-two, had taken his degree
from a small college in Louisville. The résumé listed
internships and hospital privileges in both Kentucky
and Tennessee. A few years were then unaccounted
for, but a license and three different business addresses

in North Carolina made me think he must have been struggling to find a steady practice.

It was all pretty undistinguished stuff until I got to the address listing in Moultrie, Georgia. The work address was for the State Penitentiary. His title there had been head of prison psychiatric services. He had worked there for four years. There was another lapse in time before his next official work record for Health and Prison Services of Florida. His current address was in Golden Beaches, just as McCane had said.

What McCane had not said—except to a bartender he was probably trying to hit on at Kim's—was whether he had ever been in Moultrie. I put the file down and stared out at the sun flashes on the small shore break. Coincidence that McCane had worked in the same Georgia prison as the middleman who might be killing Billy's women? Was the old cop chasing down a lead he wasn't filling me in on? How well did these guys know each other?

I was getting more coffee when my cell rang.

"Billy?" I answered.

"Richards," she said, her voice professional and with an edge.

"Hey. What's up? They call you off the homicide?"

"Freeman. Didn't you tell me at Lester's that your partner the insurance investigator was trailing some middleman?"

"Yeah, he was doing surveillance on the guy's place and trailed him to the liquor store."

"Said his name was Marshack?"

"Yeah. A psychiatrist named . . ."

"Dr. Harold Marshack," she finished my sentence. "Max, you better get down here."

I called Billy and filled him in on the homicide of Dr. Marshack, McCane's middleman and the county jail psychiatrist. Billy jumped ahead of me.

"And the Moultrie prison psychiatrist. You're thinking they knew each other?"

"Let's get the paperwork before I call McCane," I said, getting up to leave. "Call me."

When I found the address along A1A in Golden Beaches, I again pulled into a lot filled with squad cars and a couple of unmarked units parked alongside. A team of crime scene guys was going over an old-model Caprice in a spot nearby.

As I got out I could see Richards and Diaz, standing next to their boss. Hammonds cut his eyes toward me and then turned back to say something to his detectives before walking away. Richards met me halfway across the lot.

"We've got to quit meeting like this," she said, but the joke had lost some of its humor. "The boss man is hot again."

I nodded, tried to catch the color in her eyes, but gave up when Diaz joined us.

"Hey amigo. Told you we would meet again," he said, the smile undiminished. "You want to tell us again how your private investigation somehow involves the stiff we got upstairs who works for us?"

"Good to see you too, Vince," I said, before running

through the case again, only leaving out the Moultrie connection. No use throwing that in the mix until Billy had it nailed down.

"So what'd you tell Hammonds?" I asked when I was through.

"Told him everything we've got," Richards said. "The five naturals. The theory on the insurance scam. Marshack's name coming up as a possible middleman in the deal."

"And?"

She said nothing.

"And she got her ass chewed for not puttin' all that in the report on the killing at the Thompson house," Diaz said.

I looked again at Richards, who was shaking her head like it was no big deal.

"What's passed is passed," she finally said. "You're in, Max. Let's go upstairs and take a look."

"Come on, let's take a look," said Diaz, when I didn't move. "Enlighten us once again, Mr. Philadelphia."

I started to follow them to the entrance door of Marshack's building when Hammonds called out my name. He didn't move. I had to go to him.

He was a thin man, in his late fifties, and he carried the kind of attitude in statement and action that came from years of giving orders. He was in a suit, the knot of his tie cinched up tight against his throat. Our previous encounters had not been genial. He had resented what he considered my interference in his domain.

"Mr. Freeman," he said when I got close. "Bad things seem to happen around you."

No question was asked, so I didn't feel an obligation to respond.

It was an uncomfortable standoff that he finally broke. "If you plan to keep showing yourself around the county, I suggest you at least get a P.I.'s license."

Again, since a question had not been asked, I only nodded my head.

"Go take a look," Hammonds said. "And I'd rather not have you holding back on us this time."

I rejoined Diaz and Richards and shrugged. All three of us turned and continued to the front entrance.

Marshack's two-bedroom condo had been tossed. Badly. Books off the shelves. Cushions and mattress flipped. Drawers emptied and blood on the kitchen floor.

"They come up with a murder weapon?" I asked.

"Sharp end of a broken bottle," Richards said. "Hennessy Cognac."

We traded looks. I thought of McCane's suggestion of getting a warrant and searching the place. When Richards had given me the name I'd paged the insurance investigator to ask if he'd been on surveillance or just drinking last night. He hadn't called me back.

The desk against one wall of the living room had been pried open. The computer monitor was flipped on its side and the keyboard shoved aside. The hard drive was gone.

"Some old lady down the hall called nine-one-one when she heard a ruckus but she stayed behind her own locked door until the first uniform guys got here. Didn't see a thing," Diaz said.

"Print guys got a lot of latents but could all be the doc's. No jewelry that we could find, and the guy's wallet and wrist watch were missing."

"The outside doors are buzzed open after ten and the condo door wasn't jimmied or forced," Richards added. "Makes it look like he let the killer in, put up a fight, might have even broken the bottle of booze himself for protection but got it taken away and jammed in his own neck."

It was the first impression, but I wasn't going for it.

"Then the guy goes through the drawers, the files, the closets and runs out the door with what?" I said. "The wallet, okay. The jewelry, sure. But the hard drive?"

Diaz shook his head.

"How you gonna figure some psycho from the cuckoo's nest if he comes to pay back the doc for puttin' him up in Chattahoochee for a few good years of his sexual prime?" Diaz said and Richards rolled her eyes.

"And what, Vince? He goes through the files and takes the hard drive to get his name off the nut farm list?"

"Like I said," shrugged Diaz. "Cuckoo's nest."

A burglary gone bad, or a bad job of making it look like a burglary, I thought. There wasn't much to look at.

Richards put the crime scene tape back over the door when we left. In the elevators she said the M.E.

was giving a preliminary time of death of 4:00 A.M., which matched up with the 911 call.

When we got outside, Hammonds was still talking with the crime scene supervisor, going over the Caprice. When Richards shook her head he never blinked, just went on.

"The trunk lid was popped with a ball peen hammer, just punched it through," Hammonds said to all three of us when we walked up. "But it looks like he missed the false bottom in the glove box."

He held up a plastic evidence bag that held a white, printed bank envelope.

"Six hundred-dollar bills. Still crispy," he said. "The techs are going to run the prints they found inside along with the ones upstairs, but a lot of them looked smeared. We'll try to match them to prisoner files on the forensics unit first. Maybe we get lucky."

No question had been posed, so I shut up. If Richards remembered the hundred-dollar bills, she didn't say anything. When Hammonds left, both detectives walked over to Diaz's SUV.

"Hey, amigo. Thanks for the help, eh?" Diaz said. "We gotta get back to the shop."

"Call me when you hear something?" Richards said, and the look was deeply uncertain.

26

I was still leaning against my truck, looking up at the high tower of Marshack's condo building when my cell rang.

"Freeman," I answered.

"Yo, G."

I told him I wasn't with the government.

"Yeah, you said. You know where D.C. Park at?" said the voice of the leader of the three-man off-limits crew.

"I'll find it."

"Meet us there, man, we got somethin' for you."

The crime scene techs were still working the Caprice. I asked one of them for directions to the park and left.

It took me thirty minutes to get back to the zone. I could feel a tingle of adrenaline in my blood. Maybe we get lucky, I thought. The park was a small square of green along Northwest Nineteenth Street. There were a few transplanted palms and willow trees, a multicolored plastic jungle gym and three worn picnic tables. When I pulled up the place was empty except for the table in the far shaded corner. This time there were four of them.

I kept my hands out of my pockets and crossed the open grass and when I got close enough I recognized the fourth as the Brown Man.

The crew leader nodded when I stepped up. His two friends stood and took a few steps back. The Brown Man kept his head down, only looking up with his eyes.

"So, Freeman," said the leader. He had absorbed my name, filed it. "We did some of our own investigatin' an' come up wit some information might be good." He put an emphasis on the word "might" and cut a look at the Brown Man when he said it.

"The Brown here works his gig down at the dope hole, but you already know that," he continued. The dealer hadn't moved. "He been there forever an' know everybody, hear everything, an' he say nobody been talkin' bout killin' no grands over in the off-limits."

The Brown Man shook his head and said, quietly, "Tha's right."

"But he say he got somethin' on your clean bills but he need to come over here an' see who his information goin' to an' not be seen talkin' to no G by any of his dogs, you know what I mean?"

I had an idea.

"I also need somethin' in return," the Brown Man said, finally looking up at me.

All I could do was nod.

"If you after this motherfucker an' get his ass, he don't come back on my ass, right?"

I nodded again, no vocal promises.

"Cause he one scary motherfucker an' I don't need his crazy-ass trouble, right? I'm losin' steady money on this, but I might be losin' a lot more business, or so say these homies," he said, looking around.

"You have a customer who uses new hundred-dollar bills?" I asked.

He waited. Looked around, avoiding eye contact with the others.

"Junk man," he said. "Big scary lookin' dude always be pushin' his cart round town. He been buyin' dope for a long time. Dimes an' eight-balls and shit. But last year he start buyin' bundles and payin' with new Franklins. First time he give me one I had my boys run the bill down at the store see if it any good. After that, they all be clean. Most of them new."

I didn't say anything, picturing the thick figure of the man, draped in his dark winter coat, looking up into my eyes when he'd bent to pick up a can on the street that day. And I remembered the hands, huge and swollen and powerful.

"Anybody know where this junk man lives?" I asked.

"Nobody pay no attention to him," said the crew leader. "Once we start talkin' about him, everybody seen him around, but nobody know him.

"Dog here say he thinks he live with his momma somewhere's over on Washington by the river," he said, tipping his head to one of his crew. "But he ain't sure where."

The table was silent for a full minute. Nothing more was coming.

"I appreciate the help," I finally said. "You've got my cell number. If you see this junk man, call me."

"No, no, no," said the Brown Man, turning bold. "I ain't callin' nobody down on my own corner. An' that means you too, truck man. Don't be parkin' cross the street messin' wit my business no more. That's part of the deal, too."

"I'll call you, G," said the crew leader, stepping between us. "But you better come quick we find out this junk man been doin' what you say."

I was driving around the zone, aimlessly. If the dark junk man didn't know anyone was after him, maybe he'd still be on the street, doing whatever he'd been doing during the daytime for who knows how long.

I was thinking about his eyes, the dark tunnels under the shadows of his brow when he looked up and caught my own. Were they eyes that could hold the kind of remorselessness it would take to steal innocent lives for a few hundred dollars? Eyes that could look away while he crushed an old man's throat? I'd seen the eyes of killers before.

"Taking the walk" they called it in Philly, when the arrested or convicted would be walked in their shackles and cuffs from a court hearing back to the jail. They would purposely be taken across an open-air corridor so the press cameras could all get a shot. Some group of cops would always be assigned to do crowd control, holding back the TV guys who wanted to stick a mi-

crophone in the guy's face and asked the inevitable
stupid question, "Why'd you do it?"

I'd been on the detail when they walked Heidnik.
When he looked up to see who'd asked the question,
he caught my eyes as I held back the line. Just the
quick contact made a shiver flutter at the hairline on
the back of my neck. Maybe it was the knowledge that
investigators had actually talked of Heidnik's possible
cannibalism. Maybe it was just the possibility of pure
evil that made you see what couldn't humanly be
there. But neither television nor the movies ever got it
right.

While driving I had unconsciously taken myself
back into the alley behind Ms. Thompson's house
when the cell rang.

"Freeman."

"Richards," she said. "The crime scene guys got a
match off some fingerprints from the doc's car. Some
guy named Eddie Baines. He was in Marshack's forensics unit three years ago for a couple of months on a
theft charge. We got an old home address for him, and
SWAT is headed out there now. Can you meet us?"

She sounded in control, but pumped.

"Give me the address," I said.

A cop stopped me at a roadblock three blocks away
from the house. I gave the uniformed officer
Richards's name and he called it in over his radio.

"Somebody will have to take you in," he said.

Down the street the road was blocked again by two
squad cars parked nose to nose. People who had been

evacuated from their houses were milling around, talking to the cops and probably getting little answer for their questions. Another officer jogged up and told me to follow him to the command post. Richards, Diaz and two SWAT officers were working from the side patio of a small stucco house. Richards introduced me around and then filled me in.

"His place is the beige one across and to the left." I peeked around the corner. The house had a dilapidated look that followed the neighborhood trend. All the shades were down. The driveway was empty. The roof had a deep sway in the middle as if part of the air had been let out of the place.

"The phone has been disconnected for years," she continued. "Neighbors say that Eddie used to live there with his mother, but they hadn't seen either of them for quite a while."

"How old's the mother?" I asked.

"From what we know she's got to be mid to late sixties. Property records say she's owned the place for thirty years."

"What's the sheet on our guy?"

"Thirty-seven years old. Picked up a couple of times for loitering but only the one time for theft, when they say he stole some plants off a woman's carport. Low IQ. Signs of mental illness. They kept him in the forensics unit for more than thirty days to evaluate him. Nothing in the file to show they had any trouble with him there. Dr. Marshack did a preliminary workup on the guy, but when he'd served out his time they cut him loose to the streets with an appointment for follow-up at the local mental health clinic."

"And he never showed up," I said, knowing the answer. In some things, the world worked the same no matter what city you were in.

"He have any weapons charges?"

"Nothing that showed."

"So how come SWAT?"

The two guys in black never flinched.

"We got a quasi-county employee with half a bottle stuck in his neck. We got some psycho with his prints all over the inside of the victim's car. Hammonds wants this one tight and by the book," Diaz said.

All right, I thought. Show of force. Couldn't argue with that.

"They used the bullhorn on the place already. No answer. Now they got guys coming in through the alley and it's sealed from the front by a sniper," he said, pointing up to the roof over our heads.

I looked around the corner again and watched a three-legged dog limping down the middle of the empty street, snuffling the ground and then tilting its muzzle to the air trying to figure out the smell of clean leather and fresh gun oil.

"All right, detectives, we're set in the back with the door ram. Let's get this done before it gets any darker," said the SWAT lieutenant. Richards nodded her head.

The lieutenant whispered an order into his radio, and he and his partner stepped around us and out toward the street. We heard the muffled splintering of wood and then a series of shouts from the target house. Everyone seemed to hold their breath, waiting for a crack of gunfire we would all recognize and dread. A few seconds later we heard another whump from inside and then nothing.

The lieutenant spoke into his radio, and when he raised his hand and motioned us, we moved up behind him.

"All clear inside," he said. "Nobody alive."

Diaz led the way in. The SWAT team had opened the front door and we could smell the stench spilling out on the porch. An officer coming out shouldered his MP5 machine rifle and offered Richards a tin of jellied Vapo-Rub.

"Bad in there, ma'am."

She dipped a finger and dabbed it up at her nostrils. I took him up on the offer. Diaz declined.

What furniture there was inside had been shoved up against the walls. It was hot and stale and others on the team were snapping up the window shades and trying to force open the windows. The light that washed in gave the place a gray cast. The lieutenant directed us to a bedroom door just off the kitchen that had been splintered open, but as we approached, another black-suited team member opened the nearby refrigerator door and jumped back.

"Jesus Christ," he yelped.

On a bottom shelf stood a huge glass pickle jar that at first glance seemed to be full of a caramel soda that had been shaken and was fizzing over. On second look, a boil of brown cockroaches was streaming out of the jar in an effort to flee the officer's flashlight beam.

"Shut the damn door, Bennett," the L.T. snapped, and the kid slammed the door and danced into the next room.

Richards still had her eyes closed when we went into the bedroom.

"Signal seven in the closet," said the lieutenant.

I stepped forward and looked. Folded up in a small linen closet were the remains of a woman. Her gray hair was matted on skin that wasn't far from the same color. She was curled up in a fetal position and looked too small to be an adult. There was a swatch of silver duct tape wrapped around what was left of her mouth.

"Been here a while from the looks of that decomp," said Diaz.

I turned away and noticed that all the windows had been sealed with the same duct tape. The bed was still made up. But the dresser top had been cleared of anything remotely valuable.

"Let's get the M.E. out here," Richards said. "And let's call Hammonds."

27

Another twilight was spun through with red-and-blue light bars from a line of squad cars. Another visit by the M.E.'s black Suburban. Another body bag.

I leaned up against the driver's door of Diaz's SUV while Richards talked on a cell phone inside, filling her boss in on the details. I was thinking about crisp new hundred-dollar bills, doubting that they were going to find any in this house. The detectives were playing their theme: A former psych patient goes wacko for some reason, tracks down the shrink that treated him in jail and robs and kills him.

"Uh, yeah. We've got a mug shot from the jail and a physical description, sir," Richards was saying into the phone.

Diaz had turned on the overhead light in his truck and was looking through the jail and arrest reports on Eddie Baines. He handed a sheet to her.

"We've got a black male, thirty-seven years of age, approximately five-foot-ten and 250 pounds. Brown hair, uh . . . no eye color here. Some scars on his forearms, possibly knife wounds it says here, sir. No marks or tattoos.

"Yes, sir. I believe we've already got the BOLO out, sir," she said, passing the sheet back to Diaz.

I was staring down the darkened street, seeing something big and thick and menacing in the back of my head.

"Uh, no, sir, I don't believe so." She turned to Diaz. "Anything in there about a vehicle?"

"Uh, nada," he said, reading through the arrest report. "Looks like he was stopped by patrol on foot while he was pushing some kind of shopping cart. Like a junk man or something."

I reached in through Diaz's window and plucked the sheet out of his hand.

"Yo, Freeman," he snapped.

"What?" Richards said.

I read the line about the shopping cart, the description.

"He's our guy," I said, as much to myself as to them. "That's him."

The detectives were watching me.

"Um, yes, sir. Yes, Freeman, sir," Richards was saying into the phone.

An hour later we were in Hammonds's office, on the sixth floor of the sheriff's administration building. Richards had taken up a spot leaning against a bookshelf. Diaz took the most comfortable chair off to one side, leaving me with the chair directly in front of Hammonds's desk.

"All right, Freeman. Let's get past the fact that you didn't reveal information that you had. That investigative flaw is not surprising, but bolsters my assessment of your lack of professionalism. So convince me of this theory of yours."

He was up tight against his side of the desk, his palms flat together, his tie cinched up and the sleeves of his dress shirt showing an ironed crease.

I told him of the paper trail on Marshack, the confirmation that the doctor had collected the finder's fees on the South Florida viatical policies. I told him about McCane and his tailing of Marshack to the northwest side liquor store and the detail about the new hundred-dollar bills, the same kind found in Marshack's glove box.

Hammonds peaked his fingers, touching the tips on his chin. Without him asking a question, I elected to go on.

"I made some contacts in the zone and they picked up the word from one of your local drug dealers that a man fitting the description of Eddie Baines had been paying for heroin with new hundred-dollar bills."

"So we've got a psychotic with a heroin addiction walking around in Three Zone. He may or may not have been getting money for his habit from his jail psychiatrist. He may or may not have killed that psychiatrist. He also may or may not have killed his mother and left her in her closet to rot," Hammonds said, turning to Richards. "You have any reason to believe this guy has any connection with the rapes and killings you're supposed to be working, detective?"

"Location. Opportunity. Knowledge of the streets. And now, the possible propensity to violence," she said.

Hammonds let that sit for a moment.

"I ask you the same question, Mr. Freeman."

"If Marshack was paying this guy with hundred-dollar bills to get high, what was he getting in return for his money?" I said. "And if he was collecting a finder's fee on viaticals, was he lining up Baines as his hit man?"

Hammonds shook his head.

"Those aren't reasons, Freeman, they're questions," he said. "But since you have built these so-called contacts in the zone, it's my suggestion that you ride with Detective Richards and see if we might be able to find this junk man.

"And Detective Diaz. I want you to get with a computer tech and go through all the files Marshack may have had over in his office at the jail. Going on the supposition that Marshack's killer was also looking for something, let's see if what our burglar was looking for might have been stashed in a place even he couldn't get into."

We stood up and Hammonds reached for the phone and then realized that Richards hadn't moved.

"Problem, Detective?"

"Suggestion, sir. Since I'm a lot better on the computer side and Vince has patrolled that zone before, sir,

I think we'd be better served by switching the assignments, sir."

Hammonds swept us all with his gaze, as if trying to figure something out.

"Whatever it takes to get it done," he said, and dismissed us.

28

Richards avoided my eyes when we split up, her to the jail, Vince and I to the parking lot. I watched her disappear down a long hallway.

"Hey," Diaz said. "Don't let it get to you, man. She's like that all the time with all these cops trying to hit on her. More than two years her husband is dead and she's still cold, man. It's nothing personal. Women hold onto their pain."

I turned back to him.

"That's real philosophical, Vince."

"Hey," he shrugged. "I'm Cuban. I know women."

We took Diaz's SUV, the new equivalent to the old unmarked four-door Crown Victoria that used to scream "cop" to any criminal with a brain. The advantage in South Florida was that there were so many SUVs on the road they could blend in most of the time. But we still got second looks from the people hanging on the streets in the northwest zone.

"I wasn't so sure about Richards myself when Ham-

monds made us partner up," he started in again.
"Then one night we're doing a job on this place the
kids called a satanic worship site in this old shut-
down trash incinerator. I tell her to wait outside while
I check out this big empty furnace room. Inside it gets
this weird red glow when you put the flashlight on
and I'm checking this pile of melted candles and
BOOM! Some fucking psycho drops out of the ceiling
on me. Big, strong guy got a fucking tire iron, man. I'm
going oh shit and the next thing I hear is Richards
screaming, 'Freeze it up, asshole!' "

I was trying not to grin at the scene in my head.
Richards saving Diaz's ass. So I stared straight ahead
and let him finish.

"She's got the barrel of her 9mm screwed into this
guy's ear and I believed her, man. I think she would
have done the guy."

"You ease up on her after that?"

"Sure, you see how nice I am now," he said, smiling.
"I'm just warning you, man."

Diaz slowed and crawled, almost royally, down the
street that was considered the Brown Man's territory.
Two middle-aged men walking with a bag of groceries
watched us pass, not stopping but turning their heads
to follow our taillights, looking to see if anything was
going to happen.

"So we think this cat is a junkie, right?" Diaz said.
"Shouldn't be too hard to pick out if he's as big as that
report says."

"Maybe," I said.

"Maybe? Hell, guy like that everybody notices, man."

He pulled even to the Brown Man's stool, but the dealer refused to look up. Catching me off guard, Diaz hit the power button and rolled down my passenger-side window.

"Yo, Carlyle. Was up?" Diaz yelled, leaning forward to look out my window.

Again, the Brown Man didn't move his head, but his eyes did and when he saw me, he gathered the moisture in his cheek and spat in the gutter.

Diaz laughed and moved on.

"Look, Detective. I know this is your turf, but maybe it'd be a good idea if we tried to be a little less conspicuous," I said. "My sense of this Baines guy is that he moves a lot on the side streets, out of the main flow."

"Yeah, sure," Diaz said. "How 'bout we stop and get some coffee and then cruise over by his place. Maybe he's hanging around the perimeter of his momma's."

Diaz pulled into a market he called the "Stop and Rob" and I got two sixteen-ounce cups for myself and held one between my feet while sipping from the other. We drove in silence. I kept my window down, watching the sides of the streets, the activity between houses and businesses and the shadows cast by the high-density security lights in parking lots.

My old partner in Philadelphia had a habit of trying to educate me with his eclectic reading. Whenever we cruised west Philly and the hard streets were quiet, he would quote from historian Will Durant: "Civilization is a stream with banks. The stream is sometimes filled with blood from people killing, stealing, shouting and doing the things historians usually record, while on the banks, unnoticed, people build homes, make love, raise children, sing songs, write poetry and even whittle statues. The story of civilization is what happened on the banks."

My partner said that was why historians were pessimists. Historians and cops, I thought. I was starting to believe that Eddie Baines's life went on even further back from the banks, hidden back behind the tree line. And he only came into the stream to feed at its edges.

Diaz took the alleys, his headlights off, the yellow glow of his running lights spraying dull out on the garbage cans and hedges and slat fences. When we got to the block before Baines's mother's house, he stopped and pulled the SUV along the swale. From here we could see both down the alley behind the house and a piece of the street in front. I finished my first cup.

"How could somebody do that to their own mother?" Diaz said. "You know, in the Cuban culture, respect for the one who brought you into this world is an unspoken rule. You learn it as a child. And you don't forget. That's what holds us together, man, you know?"

Diaz was that kind of surveillance cop. A talker. It was the only way he could fill the long hours. I didn't mind. I'd had other partners who were the same. It was like background noise. He talked and watched. I sipped and watched.

"My own mother came to Miami on one of the first freedom flights in 1965. Only a girl. She had to leave my grandmother behind to the jackal Fidel," he said, snickering. "That's what she always called him, my mother.

"She got married over here, to another Cuban refugee, but my father was never the strong one. She was the one who learned English, got us to school, made sure we were fed, practically pushed my sister through the doors of the University of Miami."

While he talked, I thought of my own mother sitting with her rosary, the Catholic habit she couldn't give up, and how she never again slept in the bedroom she shared with my father before his death. She took my old room.

At the policeman's funeral she was silent and dressed in black. And when they presented her with a flag, still not a tear fell from her cheek. She sat at our kitchen table during the traditional family gathering afterward, as relatives moved in and out of her house, eating pastas and meatballs and cheesecakes from Antonio's Bakery.

The men, most of them cops, gathered in the backyard, quietly guffawing, beers in their hands despite the March chill. My uncle Keith would come in and rub his palms together and ask her if he could get her anything, and she would look only him in the eye and turn the rosary over in her hands and shake her head.

After they all left she rarely saw them again. When I would come on Sunday morning to drive her to First Methodist, she would still be at the table, dressed warmly, watching the dust float in the stream of early light flowing through the back window.

The only times I remember any part of a smile coming to her face was when she and Billy's mother would greet each other in the basement of the church. They would hug one another like sisters, holding hands, the contrast of my mother's now pale and blue-veined hands wrapped in the wrinkled brown of her friend's.

Within two years she was diagnosed with cancer. I took her to the doctor's and then to a clinic four times before she gave up. She simply said no more and refused to be taken from her house. Neighborhood women would bring her dishes to eat, try to sit by her side, but she would not confide in them.

When my mother became too weak, Mrs. Manchester would come on the Broad Street subway from her home in North Philly, walking the last several blocks to the house. She would clean and cook and sit with my mother for hours, reading from the Bible. The relatives and neighbors accepted the black woman's role in a house where they themselves were not invited by considering her a kind of nurse and housekeeper.

For two more years my mother hung on. Near the end I would come each evening before my night shift started and make sure she had at least eaten something. A real nurse was visiting now, someone from hospice care. They had set up a morphine drip that my mother had refused at first, but then acquiesced to out of pure weakness. I would sit by the side of her bed, the same bed I had slept in through my childhood and teenage years, and massage her legs, the only place she would admit to having pain.

She still recognized me, and when I would bring

her hand up to my cheek she would say, "Maxey, forgive me."

And I would repeat that there was nothing for me to forgive.

When she died the rest of the family was aghast when they found out that I was honoring my mother's wishes and having her cremated. She had fought through her duty to lay next to my father for too many years and did not want to do so for eternity.

It was only after she passed that my uncle Keith took me aside and told me about the arsenic poisoning. The liver failure that my father had suffered could easily have been attributed to cirrhosis, even though the medical examiner had come up with an unnatural level of arsenic in his system. Being the nature of the police club, whose circle of influence included the M.E.'s and prosecutors and neighborhood politicos, that information had been quietly buried or simply ignored. It was the first time I had to admit to the benefits of the code of silence.

"Nobody knows," said my father's only brother. "And nobody blames her for the bastard he was, God rest his soul."

Mrs. Manchester came to the funeral service, causing a whispering among the relatives and family friends who attended at the Methodist church. The old black woman sat in a back pew long after everyone else had gone. As I left, she rose and came up to me and held both of my hands and said, "God forgives."

*   *   *

It was well after midnight when Diaz called it quits.

"We ain't going to even see this junk man in the dark," he said, turning down another alley. "I say we get Bravo shift to make sure they stop by the kitchen Dumpsters in the morning, try to nab the guy diving for something to eat. The guy has to eat, no?"

I talked him into taking another swing through the alley behind the Thompson house, on a gut feeling.

"You're talking about a psycho returning to the scene of the crime, Freeman, and we don't even know for sure if this guy did the crime."

We were coming out of Ms. Thompson's alley when Diaz flipped on his headlights and the beams caught the off-limits crew huddled on the opposite corner.

"Fuck is this group of homeboys up late on a school night?" Diaz said.

"Pull up," I said.

We stopped with my window facing the crew. The leader recognized me through the open window and took a step forward. Diaz was smart enough to keep his silence.

"You teamin' up wit the five-oh, eh, G?" he said, looking past me to Diaz. "I thought you guys didn't get along, you know, all that bigfootin' shit you see on the movies."

"I'll assume you haven't got anything," I said, ignoring his act in front of Diaz.

"We got our word out. I'll call you, like I said. But you best answer quick."

I nodded and we moved on.

"That your connection, Freeman? Crew of wanna-bes working way outside the action zone?"

I didn't turn my head.

"Let's call it a night, Detective. You're probably right, you should turn that kitchen suggestion over to the daysiders."

29

Eddie was under the I-95 overpass, tucked up as high on the concrete slope as he could get. His coat was wrapped tight around him and he was shivering.

After Mr. Harold had given him two more hundred-dollar bills and promised he would meet him at the liquor store in three days, Eddie went to buy more drugs. He knew Mr. Harold would keep his promise. He hadn't seemed mad at all that Ms. Thompson wasn't dead, if that was true. Eddie had asked him if he should go again to her place on Thirty-second Avenue and Mr. Harold said no, he'd have to talk to someone else and find out what they should do. He had given him the money and even let Eddie get out of the parking lot before he started the Caprice and drove away.

Eddie had started feeling better, was getting back to his routine, pushing his cart at night when he saw the blue-and-red lights flashing down the street near his momma's house. He was coming down off a high and couldn't figure out why the police cars were pointing at each other.

From behind a hedge he watched them waving cars on when they slowed down to look. People that he recognized, neighbors of his mother, were standing near the cars, walking back and forth, asking the cops questions and then turning away in frustration. Ms. Emily was out there with her old robe and slippers on, her hair all standing up straight and stiff-like, her voice like his momma's, all high and preachy.

"Ain't nobody in that house, I'm tellin' y'all. Ms. Baines done left to go back up to Carolina to be with her people," she was singing to one of the cops. "Y'all got us standin' out here for nothin', an' I'm gonna miss my *Survivor*."

Eddie left after he heard his mother's name used. He took the alleys and the back ways and stopped once behind the auto glass place to mix his last package of heroin. Before the sun came up he was here, under the bridge.

Nearby, three homeless men were taking turns with a WILL WORK FOR FOOD, GOD BLESS YOU sign. Two would stay down under the bridge, sharing a bottle, while the third climbed up for handouts on the off ramp. When one man's allotted time was done, they would switch. When they first saw Eddie curled up, they watched him carefully, eyeing his cart down below. But when they got brave and came close, Eddie unfolded himself and stared into their faces and they backed off and went on with their routine.

Now, with the traffic humming and burring across

the concrete above him and the full sun hot just a few feet away, he was cold.

Maybe if he waited for the dark, he thought, maybe then he could be invisible again.

After Diaz dropped me at the sheriff's office, I spent the rest of the night sleeping in my truck, parked in a spot along the oceanfront. It was windless but I could still hear the surf sliding up on the wet sand. I was awake when the sky went from dark to gray to a green-blue blush, and then the sun rose like a bubble of wax. When it cleared the horizon it threw a trail of light crystals across the flat water.

My cell phone rang at 7:00 A.M.

"Sorry if I woke you at an inopportune time," Billy said. "But I did manage to get some information and I wanted to pass it on while you were in the thick of things."

"You saw the news?"

"The demise of Dr. Marshack seems particularly co-incidental, and I know how much you despise that standard."

"So spill already," I said, trying to rub my eyes into focus before realizing that there was a film of salt spread across my front window.

"Dr. Marshack did indeed work at the prison at the same time as McCane. He left a year after McCane was bounced."

"Have you talked with our partner recently?" Billy asked.

"I paged him," I said. "Nothing."

"I'll call his main office in Savannah, find out if he is still supposed to be on the job," Billy said.

When I filled him in on the way Eddie Baines was fleshing out, Billy went silent for an uncomfortable stretch.

"Nothing to tie him to the deaths of our women?"

"Nothing but a feeling, Billy. But we haven't been able to talk with him yet. I'll call you," I said and punched the set off.

The sun had gone white and the air in the cab was already thick and hot. I rolled up the window, kicked on the A.C. and went to find coffee.

I was sitting at a sidewalk table at a beachfront café watching the early sunbathers make their trek to the sand when McCane called.

"Hey, Freeman. I didn't catch you loungin' around in someone's bed this morning getting' a little on-the-job perk, did I?"

I took a long drink of hot coffee, counted five cars rolling by on the avenue and waited until my jaw un-clenched.

"Freeman? You there, bud?"

"You lose your beeper, McCane?" I finally answered.

"Nope. Got it right here with, uh, three of your pages on it."

"You been on vacation?"

"Matter of fact I was down to Miami," he said, putting a southern "ah" on the end of the city's name. "You ever been on that Miami Beach, Freeman? There is some kind of modelin' show goin' on down that

way, bud. Girls out on the sidewalk with legs right up
to their . . ."

"Spare me, McCane," I interrupted him. "You
bother checking out the news up here?"

"Well now, I did see where our Mr. Marshack
bought his. Didn't pick up quite how in the papers,
though. Kind of thing they tend to keep out, so's they
can narrow down the suspect field," he said with a
matter-of-fact tone in his voice. "But I suppose you got
the inside story since you and your detective friend
was there."

"You were watching?" I asked.

"I was just rollin' in. Was figurin' on setting up a little morning surveillance, follow the guy to work since
the night tail wasn't getting me much."

"So you weren't there overnight?"

"Unfortunate," he said. "Your friends got any suspects?"

I didn't answer, wondering who it was that McCane
might be tailing now since the doctor was no longer
available.

"It might be a good idea if you and I get together
and put some of these pieces together, McCane. If
you're not too busy, I'm thinking Mr. Manchester's office this afternoon?"

"All right, bud. I got a few errands to run. But why
don't ya'll set it up and page me with a time."

After McCane hung up I sat finishing my coffee, and
watched a girl across the street on rollerblades take an
ugly tumble on the sidewalk. A few other morning
walkers stopped to help her up and even from here I

could see a bright pink oval of blood on the side of her knee that had been sandpapered off by the concrete. While the small commotion attracted attention I put my money under my empty cup and slipped away, watching carefully for any parked cars nearby, looking for a single man sitting in the driver's seat.

I was back in my truck, just easing into traffic when the phone rang again.

"Freeman."

"Good morning. Heard you and Diaz had a wonderful time last night," Richards said.

"Yeah, a true conversationalist, that partner of yours," I said.

"If you haven't had breakfast yet, can you meet me over at Lester's?"

I'd spent the night in my car and looked like hell. In the rearview mirror it was even worse.

"Yeah, sure," I said. "What have you got?"

While I was stopped on the causeway waiting for the Intracoastal drawbridge to let a high-masted sailboat through, she told me of her excursion into Dr. Marshack's computer files at the jail.

It had taken some time to convince a judge to allow them access.

The city attorney argued that it was vital to a homicide investigation and that the hardware and software was already under the sheriff's control in their own facility. The judge countered that many of the files were psychiatric records that held a certain doctor and patient confidentiality.

"They finally agreed to have a court-appointed attorney look over our shoulder so that the patient files wouldn't be perused."

"Even Baines's?"

"Especially Baines's."

"So we got nothing?"

"On Baines we got nothing, but there was an interesting file in the hard drive that our tech guys had to hack into to get open. It's some kind of financial accounting of transactions between Marshack and someone or something called Milo."

She waited for some kind of response.

"Max?"

I was staring at a blinking yellow light on the bridge tower when the irritated punch of a horn snapped me back. The gates were up, cars were moving.

"Does that mean anything to you? Milo?"

"*Catch-22*," I said.

"Huh?"

"Did you print that out?"

"Sure. I've got it right here," she said.

"I'll meet you at Lester's."

When I walked into the diner, she was already in the back booth.

"Freeman, you look like sin."

"Thank you," I replied.

I could feel the beard bristles on my face. My non-wrinkle canvas pants were wrinkled. And I could feel a sheen of salted moisture on my skin.

I sat down heavily in the booth opposite her and coffee seemed to appear beside my elbow.

"You're not so fresh yourself," I said. The whites of her eyes had taken on a pink glow in the corners where several veins had gone red. She wasn't wearing any makeup and her hair was pulled up and knotted in a loose ponytail.

"It took most of the night for the techs to pull all of this stuff out of Marshack's hard drive," she said, pushing a folder of computer printouts across the table. "They figured that since this file was so well-protected it must have some meaning to it. What the hell did you mean by *Catch-22*?"

She had already ordered me pancakes, and they came while I started sorting through the columns of dates and rows of figures. The smell caused me to start absentmindedly cutting them with a fork and eating.

"Old Joseph Heller book," I said. "It's where they got the phrase. This bomber crewman is trying to prove he's crazy by flying these dangerous missions in WWII. But the fact that he keeps going up proves he's not crazy because he can still do his job. But if he refuses to go up, it proves that he realizes how crazy it is, so again he's not crazy."

"Never read it," Richards said. "And what's it got to do with Milo?"

I washed another mouthful down with coffee.

"Milo was a character in the book. A G.I. who was making a killing swapping out government supplies for illicit civilian goods. Billy tracked down McCane's work history and found out he worked in a Georgia prison and lost his job for running scams inside on the population."

"Yeah," Richards said. "Keep going."

"McCane and Dr. Marshack worked in the same prison at the same time. A prosecutor friend of Billy's said McCane was like the operator inside. You needed it, McCane was the bull to get it through. I took a chance on a guy I knew who'd been sent to the place and he used McCane's nickname, Milo. Said McCane was proud of it."

I let her digest the information while I was matching up the dates that Marshack had recorded apparent payouts with the time of death dates for Billy's women. They were close.

"If you fill in the blanks, Marshack was paying somebody three hundred dollars a few days before each death and two hundred dollars afterwards," I said, pointing out the figures. "Then within two weeks, he was getting eight thousand dollars from Milo."

"Tight little business," she said. "But if McCane is Milo, how much was he getting? And from where?"

"The investment group," I said. "With at least three people between them and the killer. And each of them set apart on a need-to-know basis. If McCane set this up, he wouldn't know who the hit man was, and Marshack wouldn't know who the investors were."

I reached for my coffee but Richards was just finishing the last of it.

"So you're figuring the psychotic patient, Baines, for the killer," she said. "But the last one didn't work the way they wanted it to, and your friend Billy had already stirred up the nest by looking into the other deaths."

I stood up and snapped the cell phone off my belt.

"I've got to let Billy know," I said. "We're supposed to meet with McCane this afternoon."

I got Billy at his office and ran through the ledger file and the Milo connection and told him to stall McCane if he called.

"Not a problem," Billy said and then went silent. I knew my friend, knew those silences meant he was trying to collect a thought, pare it down before putting it into words.

"What? All this doesn't surprise you, counselor?"

"I've been trying to track Marshack's stolen hard drive," he said, finally letting it go.

"Yeah. So's every cop with a pawn shop connection."

"Might not be in a pawn shop. If the killer needed to find out what was inside, he'd take it to a hacker who could get into it. A hacker who wouldn't tell what he found or who he found it for."

"Ideas?" I said.

"I've been thinking maybe someone who was very good with computers who'd stretched themselves in an insurance fraud and might have come into contact with an insurance investigator."

"Jesus, Billy. You found someone who McCane's company nailed for hacking?"

"Not yet. I'm working on it, but Sherry might be able to help us if they've got a computer crime investigator with a good memory."

I handed the phone to Richards and sat staring out into the sunlight flashing off the chrome and glass in

the parking lot, letting them talk, my head gone to another place.

Richards closed the phone and slid out of her side of
the booth.

"So what did he say?"

"He thinks if he can track our dead doctor's computer to McCane, then it's a lock that McCane took out
Marshack to cover any link to your women," she said.
"He's got access to the insurance company files and
we've got access downtown to all the known hackers
who've been snagged in the past few years. It'll be
faster if we work together."

I got out of the booth and took a fold of money out
of my pocket, looking at the denominations.

"Max. If you guys are right on this McCane guy, and
I'm not so sure you are, then it's a race for Baines."

I was still looking at my money.

"And if you're wrong and this guy is legit, then . . ."

"Then it's still a race," I interrupted.

30

I drove back into the off-limits zone. My posse had been good to me once. They knew the streets. Their chances of digging out the junk man were better than anyone's. I was looking for them when I pulled onto Ms. Thompson's street. Their shady spot on the corner was empty. But when I passed the Thompson house, a rental car was parked in the swale instead of up in the empty driveway. I realized that in my earlier meetings with McCane I had never seen the kind of car he was driving and wondered if it had been intentional. The easier to tail you with, bud.

I pulled up in front of the rental, nose to nose, and got out. I was shifting into cop mode, tasting a bubble of adrenaline in my throat. Thrill of the chase, a thrill I once wanted to believe I could leave in the past.

Ms. Thompson's house had a southern exposure and the sun was bright on the front windows. As I walked up I couldn't see any movement behind them. The front door was closed tight and I stood there for a second, listening. I instinctively reached down to my hip but my 9mm had long been retired. After the ranger shootings the gun had been retrieved from the river and bagged as evidence. I had never asked for its return.

I knocked. It was quiet. I knocked a second time and this time I heard a shrill but composed answer come from around the corner.

"Round back here. On the patio," came the old woman's voice.

I passed through the open carport and found them there, McCane and Ms. Thompson, sitting at a wrought-iron table, cups of coffee before each of them. An old photo album was opened between them.

Ms. Thompson looked at me and I could tell from her eyes that she was searching to recognize where she had seen me before. McCane saw it, too.

"Well, Mr. Freeman. What a pleasant surprise," he said, pushing his chair back. "Ms. Thompson, this is Mr. Max Freeman, an associate of mine. I believe you two may have met the day of your very unfortunate situation."

He smiled up at me, showing his big, blocked teeth. I could imagine it had been a false smile seen by many clients and inmates in the past.

"Why yes, I do believe I recall now," said Ms. Thompson, who had lost some of her rough exterior in McCane's presence. "Would you care to join us, Mr. Freeman? Mr. McCane has stopped by to discuss an insurance policy I have with ya'll's company, but we have been a bit sidetracked on this lovely day."

"No doubt," I said, looking from one to the other.

"May I get you some coffee, Mr. Freeman?" she said, starting to get up.

"No, please, don't bother yourself," I said, but she was already motioning me to sit.

"It is never a bother to be a gracious hostess, sir," she said, moving slowly toward her back door.

"Thank you, ma'am."

I continued to stand, putting my back to the house and facing McCane. He crossed his thick ankles and did not look up.

"Y'all didn't do much of a job interviewing Ms. Thompson here," he started, slipping back into his good ol' boy cant. "You and your detective girlfriend ought to learn how to lay on a little sugar when you're trying to get something out of these folk."

"Do tell," I said.

"Specially the old ones. Trick is to get them using their memories to kind of loosen their stopped-up brains a little. Oh yes, we been reminiscin' 'bout old times, all her pickaninnies and her poor deadbeat husband.

"Hell, she even pulled out the old pictures here," he said, touching the photo album with the blunt tips of his fingers. "Showed me the one of her mother sittin' at a nightclub in Overtown with Cassius Clay long before he become the droolin' and shakin' poster boy for the Olympics."

The adrenaline had soured in my mouth and been replaced by a warm anger that was spreading into my neck. Still he did not look up.

"So the old lady didn't see a damn thing the night

her boyfriend got his throat crushed. But she did recall smelling something, Freeman. You've got to remember all the senses in this line of work, bud," he said.

"She smelled the garbage can in her bedroom after he left is the way she put it. And a man's hand pushin' down on that pillow that had to be the size of a big 'ol catcher's mitt how it fit over her entire face and head.

"That fit with anybody you and your girlfriend been trackin'?"

I was counting to myself again, swallowing a growing rage.

"You've been tailing us, McCane. You see anybody that you were hoping we'd lead you to?" I said.

He continued to smear his fingers on the plastic cover of the album.

"No. I didn't think so," I answered myself. "If you had, you wouldn't be here."

Richards had been right getting Hammonds to call in an overtime squad to step up the BOLO on Baines while she and Billy tried to get a lock on the doctor's hard drive.

Ms. Thompson reappeared and McCane stayed quiet. She put a cup down in front of the empty chair and said, "Oh mercy, I have forgotten our milk, Mr. McCane. Please, please, sit down Mr. Freeman. I'll be right back."

McCane took a long sip of his black coffee while the woman tottered away.

"You ought to know by now, Freeman. These are just simple minds you're dealing with."

"And you ought to know how to manipulate them, Milo, considering the practice you've had," I said, holding his eyes and watching the twitch behind them at the mention of his old prison nickname. He sat quiet for a minute, glancing out toward the alley.

"I see your boy Manchester been busy checking my past," he said, trying to sound unfazed.

"And your boy Marshack's, too," I said. "You have some interesting coffee hours up at the Georgia state pen?"

He surprised me with a short laugh that came from deep in his chest.

"Ol' doc, he never was one for small talk, always pullin' that philosophical shit on you, trying to impress how smart he was. But the boy just could not hold a job," he said. "You know how far a guy gotta tumble to end up being a shrink in a prison?"

"I wouldn't know, McCane, but the good doctor sure did know how to keep some damned immaculate records. And if they tie you to it, McCane, the cons at Moultrie are going to throw an interesting homecoming."

My words stole the smugness from his face. I could see his knuckles whitening around the coffee cup. Again he cut his eyes to the hedges along the back lawn where some movement seemed to have caught him.

"Well, gentlemen. Excuse my absence," Ms. Thompson said, stepping carefully onto the patio. She froze when she saw the look on our faces.

"Get your ass back inside, old woman," McCane snapped, pushing his chair back and standing.

The words were like a slap and a warning that I had gone too far. Don't put him in a corner, I thought.

"Well, I never," Ms. Thompson spouted, starting to get her feistiness back. But I looked in her eyes and she saw a warning there. She'd seen enough in her years to keep from getting between two angered men. She turned, hissing, and retreated back into her house.

I watched McCane pulling himself back down, the flex of the hand, the loosening of the jaw. He started to chuckle.

"Freeman, Freeman, Freeman. You are some kinda big city detective, bud, with all this conspiracy talk. Hell, I thought I was just helpin' you boys out down here, and now you all cookin' up this wild-ass conjecture."

He was shaking his head. The ol' southern boy perplexed by it all.

"Hell, if that's the way it is, Freeman, I will be glad to get on back to the home office and leave this all to you smart folks," he said, getting up with a bemused look on his face.

"I'm glad you can find the humor in it, McCane. You may very well be right," I said, moving past him toward the side of the house, hoping he would follow me into the open.

"I'm sure you've got all your financials in shape. Money in, money out. Your salary from the insurance company will match up with all your expenditures. You know how these things go, McCane—follow the money."

"But you haven't done any of that yet, have you, Freeman?" he said, moving up behind me. I could feel his closeness, hear the heavy shoes shuffling in the blades of grass. "And your boy can't get that kind of information without a subpoena, and you don't get that without an official investigation. And from what I seen, you're far from official, bud."

"It would probably be a hell of a lot easier on you, McCane, if it didn't get that official."

I'd turned to him and was walking backward now, holding his eyes as we came around the corner of the house to the front lawn. Then I saw his face change.

When I looked around, the three street guardians were leaning up against the rental car. The leader in the middle, his head turned down, watched our approach from under the edge of a Marlins' ball cap. He was poking at his teeth with a toothpick. His friends had their hands in their pockets. While I hesitated, McCane stepped past me.

"Get y'all dusty asses off my car, niggers," he said, striding toward the group.

Without a word all three of them nonchalantly flexed their leg muscles and bent forward, bouncing their rumps off the fenders and taking one step forward. Their eyes followed McCane as he passed them and walked around to the driver's side.

McCane got in, started the car and pulled around my truck, driving slowly and with as much dignity as one could in a tiny rental. We all watched him turn the first corner and disappear.

"Tell me that cracker cop ain't workin' wit you, G," said the leader without turning to me, his words directed in the direction of McCane's car.

"He's not working with me," I said.

"Then what's he doin' round Ms. Thompson's?"

It was my turn to hold a response.

"I think he's looking for the junk man," I finally said.

The leader was quiet while he poked at an upper tooth.

"Ahh," he said, a grin pulling at the corners of his mouth. "A unified goal."

"You call me if you find him," I said, climbing into my truck.

Eddie was out in the street. He couldn't wait under the bridge forever. He had two more days to wait out Mr. Harold, and the ache in his veins was too much. He needed his heroin.

He had waited in his concrete corner through the daylight hours, listening to the cars overhead, trying to ignore the twisting in his stomach and the ache in his muscles. Just after nightfall, he heard the voices of the homeless men nearby, and their tone sounded oddly satisfied. He uncurled himself and approached them. He could smell gravy.

Three men were crouched in a huddle with white Styrofoam boxes in front of them. They looked up when Eddie came close. The light from the overpass lamps kept his face in darkness and cast a shadow large enough to cover them all.

"You can go down to the Salvation Army yonder and get you some," one offered, pointing to the east with a plastic fork.

Eddie stood silent. He had never gone to the feeding programs anywhere in the city. He'd seen the men, sometimes women and kids, lining up when the traveling kitchens stopped in the park on the west side. But he stayed away, his momma's voice in his head: "We ain't no welfare case, an' we don't take nothin' that ain't our deservin'." Eddie didn't try to figure why then she mostly took her dinner at the church in the last few years. "That's from God," she would say, bringing home leftovers. "And we are all deservin' from God."

Eddie determined that he was hungry now, and took a step closer to the men. When the headlights of a tractor-trailer swept through the bushes and momentarily lit his face, the three men got up and backed away, leaving their meals behind.

After he had eaten Eddie sidestepped his way down the steep embankment to his cart. He still had a hundred-dollar bill deep in his pocket, and he needed his bundle. One bundle would get him through, he convinced himself. Just one until Mr. Harold came again.

The thought of the heroin had warmed his veins and set him to pushing up the empty street toward the train station that was always empty at night. From there he could slip into the neighborhood, where he would again be invisible. And now he was out in the street.

31

Someone had put Springsteen on the jukebox. Billy was drinking a bad Merlot. Richards was sipping on a glass of white wine and I was studying a green bottle of beer that had long ago lost its soggy label. On Richards's suggestion, we were sitting in a booth at a cop bar named Brownie's.

I'd spent the day on the streets looking for the dark shape of Eddie Baines. I tried to think like him, a man who could hide himself out in the open, someone who worked in the corners of a neighborhood where he both belonged and didn't belong. The crime scene guys at the Baines house had found signs that someone had been there. Food crumbs that were new, scuffings on the dusty floors that showed the drag of a heavy boot. What was in a man's head who could bind his mother and leave her in a closet to rot?

With no authority and carrying the obvious white man's presence in a racial community, I'd poked through an abandoned bus depot near the interstate. I had introduced myself to an ancient man with a face creased and dry like dark and weathered leather at the local recycling shop. I walked the edges of the park and pulled up at the rear of the small local groceries, studying the knots of men with yellowed eyes who looked up first with anticipation and then turned away, waiting for the sound of my door opening and the yelp of some command. When I got out and showed the booking photo of Baines to a group of men playing dominoes at a corner park, they simply stared through the square of glossy paper and shook their heads. Three times during the day and into the night I'd crossed paths with patrol cops doing the same thing I was. Word had been passed at their shift briefings that I was a P.I. working the case independently. At dusk the one called Taylor crossed me at a four-way stop, pulling his cruiser into the middle of the intersection where he sat for several seconds, blocking my way, looking with a blank face into my windshield before slowly moving on.

With Billy feeding her insurance information and his own list of computer acquaintances, Richards and a BSO computer-crime expert named Robshaw had spent the day looking for someone who they could muscle into admitting they'd downloaded a stolen hard drive for a big, drawling ex-cop looking for anonymity.

Everyone was exhausted by our collective lack of success.

"We did six guys in Miami, eight here in Broward and at least that many in Palm Beach," Richards said.

"Hell, we've got as many ex-con hackers as we've got bank heist guys."

"One of our l-leads is living in a two-story b-beach house overlooking the Gulf in K-Key Largo," Billy said, keeping his voice purposely low in a public place.

"A man with a briefcase can steal more money than any man with a gun," I said to no one in particular.

Richards's eyes grinned with recognition of the song lyric. Billy just frowned.

"Don Henley, 1989," I said. My friend just shook his head.

"Diaz and his guys already confiscated a dozen computers from the local pawn shops trying to find some crackhead who might have done Marshack, but the chances are slim on that side," Richards said.

Her eyes were red-rimmed and the irises had faded to gray and I tried to catch them with my own when she locked onto something over my shoulder.

I turned and saw Hammonds making his way to the bar. Several of the officers in the place instinctively turned away from him, all of them losing two inches of height as their necks disappeared into their shoulders. It was nearly midnight, but the chief was still in his suitcoat. The knot of his tie had not been loosened.

"Give me a couple of minutes," Richards said, sliding out of her side of the booth.

I watched her move across the room and stop at Hammonds's side, and the two of them stood at the bar and leaned into their elbows for a guarded conversation.

"You know the history b-behind this p-place?" Billy said, and I shook my head, knowing he did. There was age in the wood of the long, standard bar. The ceilings were low and the wall paneling knotted and lacquered.

"In the 1930s there was a live band performing every Saturday in the back," he explained, tipping his head to a door that opened up onto the parking lot. "It w-was an open air d-dance floor and drew a young crowd. S-Some of the old-time attorneys tell about s-seeing Duke Ellington, Count Basie and Ella Fitzgerald here. At the t-time, black performers were n-not allowed to play at white d-dances in Dade County. To m-make the trip worthwhile the traveling acts would book p-places like this."

I looked around. On this night the ethnic mix looked pretty broad. But I could tell from the body language, haircuts and conversation that most of them were the same color: blue. I had spent a lot of nights in the same kind of bars in Philly.

Richards came back and slid in next to me.

"The chief says Robshaw has a lead on a hacker in Miami. Guy got busted a couple of years ago on a case where some CEO type had dipped into the corporate piggy bank to buy some expensive artwork, then later reported it stolen and tried to collect the insurance. He hired the hacker to do some eraser work on the company computers.

"Hacker flipped on the CEO but still had to do some time. They're trying to track an address on him now."

I turned to get a look at Hammonds but he had already disappeared, a full glass of beer left untouched on the bar where he'd been standing.

When I looked back at Richards she held my eyes.

"He's also opening investigations on our elderly women. He's sending crime scene teams back out to their homes with explicit instructions to check the metal jalousie tabs for any stress bends."

Billy leaned in.

"I m-might help you w-with the insurance connection. You can get the file on this hacker?"

"I told him that and he said you're free to call Robshaw and coordinate with him," Richards said.

Billy flexed his fingers and his eyes started to dart. I'd seen him get cranked before with the possibility of a challenge.

"If you w-will excuse me, f-folks," he said moving to get up. "I must go b-before they start p-playing Jimmy Buffett.

"I will be up," he said to me. "Just call."

A fresh beer had appeared and I filled half of my glass. Richards finished the wine.

"You stink, Freeman," she finally said.

There was a pull at the corner of her mouth.

"You are correct," I answered. I had been wearing the same clothes for two days, slept and sweated in them.

"How about a shower and a couple hours sleep?"

"Deal," I said, putting money on the table and following her out the door.

32

I followed her to her house and was sitting on the same steps in her backyard, watching the light from the pool dance in the tree leaves and holding a warm cup of coffee. The night was windless and still.

I closed my eyes for the fourth time in ten minutes and chastised myself for letting my head drift back to Philadelphia. Time after time I had questioned why I'd followed my father's path into this kind of work, knowing that something would happen to make it all feel like a bad mistake. When Richards came back out onto the patio, I realized my fingers had gone to the scar on my neck, and I dropped my hand.

"Your turn," she said, sitting down beside me, wrapping a long robe around her knees.

Her feet were bare and the smell of fresh soap and the assumption that she was naked under the robe started my blood moving, and I shifted my weight uncomfortably.

"Stay to your right down the hall, first door," she

said, and her eyes looked dark and oddly expression-less in the aqua light.

I passed her my half-full cup and got up saying, "I hope you left some hot water."

She had left most of the house dark. A light over the stove in the open kitchen illuminated some hanging pots and reflected off the ceramic-tiled countertop. There was a small light glowing red on the instant cof-fee maker. I thought of my own crude pot in the shack, and I was jealous.

Down the hall the bathroom light left a patch on the wooden floor. I tried to steal a look into the far bed-room door but it was too dark.

The bathroom was standard except for the modern, glassed-in shower that Richards and her husband must have installed in the old house. She'd left a fresh towel and a dark blue T-shirt, size XL, folded up on a wicker clothes basket. On top of the shirt was a can of shaving gel and a man's razor. I hurried through the shower and scraped off my stubble while I stood in the spray.

When I came back outside she was still sitting, her chin on her knees, staring into the pool water. But when she heard my steps she got up and met me halfway across the patio and stepped into my arms. Her hair was wet and cold against my cheek and I could feel her shivering against me.

She kept her head down against my chest and I lost track of time and when she finally moved it was not toward the hammock, but instead she laced her fingers into mine and led me back into the house.

* * *

Eddie was crouched in the bushes, obscured by the oak tree where the man in the blue pickup had been, watching the Brown Man do his business.

The rhythm was here. The same runners. The same hangers on. The girl with the tears and the ratty-ass mouth was hanging at the end of the block. But this time Eddie was scared. He had seen three police cars on his way here. One, parked in an alley that Eddie often used, had surprised him as he swung the corner. He had jolted to a stop only twenty feet away. But they still had not seen him, or cared if they did, he thought. Still, he had ditched his cart after that, putting it behind a Dumpster, and then moved mostly through yards and along fence lines.

Now it was late. The Brown Man would not stay out much longer and Eddie would be stuck without his bundle. The cramps were getting worse. He couldn't keep his eyes from watering or the inside of his mouth from going dry. He reached deep into his pocket and felt the hundred-dollar bill there and when the traffic stopped, he stepped out to cross the street.

The Brown Man saw him coming, raised his head when Eddie was halfway across the street, and started shaking it back and forth. Eddie came on.

The dealer hissed at him when Eddie stepped into his swale. His runners had not recognized the junk man at first without his cart, but when they did, they stayed away, having been told not to mess with him.

"Get the fuck outta here, man."

The Brown Man spit out the words and the runners

turned their heads at the sound of both the agitation and the strange hint of fear in the dealer's voice.

"You nothin' but trouble, junk man. Take your raggedy ass someplace else to get your shit."

Eddie stopped, confused. He cut his eyes to either side, saw no one who looked like they might be the police and then stared back at the Brown Man. The dealer could not hold his eyes.

Eddie reached into his pocket and held out the hundred-dollar bill, but the action just seemed to agitate the Brown Man more.

"Goddammit, nigger. Put that shit away. I ain't need your money no more. Find some other chump to do your bidness with. I'm serious now," he said, and the runners watched as the dealer slid off his stool and stood up.

Eddie saw the man's hand go to his waistband and watched the gun come out. The Brown Man held it close to his stomach so only he could see it. Eddie had seen lots of guns and had never been scared of them. The hundred-dollar bill was still in his outstretched hand. He had come for what he needed. And Eddie always got what he needed.

"A bundle," he said, stepping forward and looking into the Brown Man's face.

"You fuckin' crazy?" the dealer yelled, this time the fear in his voice scaring his own runners. "You some kinda retard?"

The gun was pointed at Eddie this time, but then the big man's other hand snapped out and swallowed the weapon and pulled the dealer into his chest.

The two men were locked into a tight, hissing dance, and the runners started to jump to the aid of their boss but froze when they heard the gun's muffled explosion. When a second shot sounded, the dealer squealed and fell away, holding his curled hand to his hip.

Eddie looked down at him and then at the gun in his own hand and then turned and tossed the piece clattering across the concrete.

The runners did not move. Not a single light came on along the street. Eddie looked up into the faces of the Brown Man's boys until they backed down and then he turned and limped away, a bloodstain growing at his side.

The feel of her leg moving off mine started me awake. She sat up, and the shift of weight on the mattress was something I had not felt in years. When I opened my eyes I could see the outline of her hip and the curve of her shoulder in the light of a still-lit candle.

Then I caught the muffled electronic ring of a phone.

"It's not mine," she said, turning from the nightstand.

"Then let it go," I said, and reached out to touch her back with my fingertips. The ringing stopped.

"See?"

She was quiet, and raised a single finger.

The ringing began again.

"Shit," I said, getting up and walking naked through another man's house and finding my phone on the porch, wrapped in a bundle of my dirty clothes.

"What?" I snapped into the mouthpiece.

"Your motherfuckin' boy busted my damn hand," came the shouted answer.

"Who the hell is this?"

"I knew they was gonna be trouble. Soon as those dogs from the other side come askin' bout hundred-dollar bills I knew I shoulda kept my mouth shut."

"Is this Carlyle?" I asked, putting it together.

"Don't you call me that," he snapped. "Your got-damn junk man done come over here lookin' for trouble and I shot his ass up."

"He's there? You killed him?" I said, trying now to keep my voice controlled.

"I didn't kill the motherfucker. He come round tryin' to buy more shit and I tried to chase his ass off and the simple motherfucker done grabbed at my piece and it went off into his own damn belly."

"Is he still there?" I repeated.

"Hell no, he ain't here. He ran his ass down the road."

"You hurt?"

"Damn right. Dude's got hands like a damn vise, man. He crushed every fuckin' bone in my hand."

"Alright. Call nine-one-one. Call an ambulance and I'll be right there."

"I ain't callin' nobody. You get that fool's ass or I waste him my own self, know what I'm sayin'?"

"Right," I said and hung up. I was standing on Richards's back porch, naked in the moonlight with a cell phone and a shiver that had just started down my back.

33

Richards called in the shooting to dispatch while we both dressed.

"No report, not even an anonymous call on gunshots fired," she said, pulling a T-shirt over her head and then grabbing her radio and a holstered 9mm from the nightstand drawer. While she locked the house I went out, started my truck and then opened the passenger door when she came out through the gate.

When we got to the dope hole, two patrol cars were spinning their lights, a shift sergeant was on the scene, and the Brown Man was gone. The sergeant was pacing the sidewalk, and the Brown Man's stool was lying tipped over in the grass. I could see another uniformed cop standing on the porch of a nearby house, speaking through a barely cracked front door.

"Good morning, Detective," the sergeant said as Richards approached.

"Sergeant Carannante," she answered. "Anything?"

"Nothing but your call, Detective. Unusually quiet

251

for a Saturday night, but the trade usually ends at mid-night or so."

The sergeant was a thick, Italian-looking man with an insouciant demeanor that said he'd seen it all before. He took me in with his eyes and did not bring them back to Richards until he was introduced.

"Uh, Max Freeman," Richards said. "He's been working with us on a case."

Carannante shook my hand.

"OK. Nice to know who's on the field," he said and turned back to her.

"Street was empty when the first unit got here. We swept the area best we could and then came back to see if we could pick up something with the flashlights. No blood spots, no shell casings, nothing. I got unit nineteen doing a canvass of residents who of course haven't seen or heard anything. And I sent another car to our man Carlyle's to see what's what."

He was a veteran cop. Giving the facts, not passing judgment on the call or the possibility that violence had occurred. Richards was herself looking unsure.

A hiss came from Carannante's radio and he spoke back, then walked back toward the patrol car. I stepped over to the toppled stool, then took a few steps further and looked across the street. I was standing on the spot where Eddie Baines had stood the first time I had met his eyes.

"Walker!" the sergeant yelled past us, signaling the cop on the porch and then moving with a purpose toward his own car.

"Dispatch says twenty-seven Bravo has spotted a big guy pushing a cart over by the river where, what, this guy Baines left his mother for dead?" It was half report, half question and directed at Richards.

"Going home to lick his wounds?" she questioned right back.

"Let's roll over there. If it's him they're going to need help throwing a perimeter," Carannante said. The cop named Walker jumped into the other squad car. "The initial report was that he could be armed. Right?" said the sergeant, again asking Richards.

She nodded and watched both cars spin U-turns and head north, their blue and red lights still throwing color on the building fronts, their sirens silent.

"Let's go, Max," Richards said.

I was looking down the street, watching the corner of a fence that led to an alley about a block down. I raised my hand and heard her footsteps behind me.

"What is it?"

"Wait a second," I said, not turning.

The block stayed quiet. Windows stayed dark. I watched the alley entrance.

"We need to go, Max. If they corner Baines we need to be there."

"Yeah, I know, just give me a minute."

She didn't sigh in resignation, or huff in exasperation. There was an element of trust going on.

We were standing in the swale, just behind my truck. I crouched down and sat on my heels and Richards followed. In less than a minute there was movement at the fence. I could pick up the light-colored material of clothing, then watched someone moving our way. There was a stumble, and a girl's quiet curse.

When we stood up she yipped in surprise, her hand to her mouth, and then started to spin away on her blocky shoes. Richards snapped, "Hold it." The girl was experienced enough to freeze.

We flanked her and she was looking defiantly at me when Richards flashed her badge.

"We're police officers," she said. "We're not going to hurt you."

"No shit," the girl said.

She was the young woman I had seen before, the one who the Brown Man had slapped across the face, the one who had spat at the feet of the junk man. She was wearing the same summer skirt but had changed her shirt.

"Have you been around all night?" I asked.

"No, I been at church all night with my girlfriends workin' the brownie sale," she said, folding her arms over her skinny chest, challenging me with her eyes.

"You didn't see your friend the Brown Man tonight?" I tried again.

"Carlyle? That fool ain't no friend of mine," she spat. "Juss a punk think he all high and mighty cause he got the franchise on the block."

She had raised her voice but then looked past us both, nervous at her own words thrown out in the dark. I reached out and grabbed her upper arm and spun her around to face me and her eyes went big.

"Ditch the attitude," I said. "You were here when Carlyle shot the junk man. What happened?"

She looked down at my hand and winced and I tightened the grip.

"She's the cop, I'm not," I said. "I don't need to worry about how I get my answers. What the fuck happened?"

The girl tried to catch Richards's eyes for some kind of protection, but she had turned away.

"Wasn't no shootin'. Not like a real one anyways," she finally said. "The junk man got in Carlyle's face an' when Carlyle got his gun out to scare him this nigger goes an' grabs it and they was both standin' there when it goes off. Then Carlyle goes down on the ground whinin' and cryin' 'bout how his damn hand was busted."

"And the junk man has the gun?" Richards said, now moving in to team up on the girl.

"No," the girl said. "He throwed it in the street an' one of Carlyle's boys went an' snatched it up."

"Where did the junk man go?"

She hesitated, looking down the street.

"He was draggin' hisself that way," she said, nodding south.

"He was wounded?" Richards asked.

"Mighta been," she said, gaining back some bravado in her voice. I squeezed the arm tighter.

"Where did he go?" I shouted.

"I didn't follow him," she said defensively. "He probably go where he always go." Tears were now coming to her eyes. "He probably go down the block-house where he always go."

Richards looked up at me and I eased off my grip on the girl's arm.

"Are you sure?" Richards asked the girl quietly. "Are you positive? Did he push his cart down there?"

"He didn't have no cart with him this time. He was draggin' his leg an' he saw me lookin' and axed me would I help him and he had a hundred-dollar bill so I helped him down at the blockhouse an' ran out of that place," she said, unable to remember her own lies.

"This is the old concrete utility room down off Thirteenth?" Richards asked.

"Yeah, where all them girls always be gettin' hurt," she said, her voice now quiet and young and sorry.

I opened the tailgate of my truck and guided her to sit. Richards was trying to raise someone on her radio.

"I already tol' that other cop where he gone," the girl said.

"What other cop?" I said. "The sergeant?"

"No, not the one with the uniform," she said. "The big ol' cracker cop been sneakin' around watchin' everybody."

Richards and I looked at each other.

"When?" Richards said. This time she grabbed the girl by the arm. "When did you tell this cop?"

"Just before you all jumped out and scared me. He come up after all the police cars got here," the girl said, turning her head to look back toward the corner where she'd been hiding.

I handed Richards my truck keys.

"You've got to hold on to her. She's a witness," I said and started walking south.

"Max, goddammit, wait for backup, Max," Richards yelled.

"And make sure you get that hundred-dollar bill for evidence, too," I said before jogging into the darkness.

34

Eddie was on the blockhouse mattress, bleeding and mumbling. The gunshot wound in his side was bearable. Eddie had a way with pain, to deal with it by keeping it out of his head. The blood had soaked through the bottom part of his T-shirt and had turned the material of his dungarees wet and dark down to the hip. But he found a ragged piece of clothing some junkie had left behind and pressed it into the spot and then leaned against the wall. He could ignore it by thinking about the girl.

After the Brown Man had shown him the gun, after he'd crushed the dealer's hand, squeezing the bones around the metal of the gun until they crinkled and snapped under his own palm, after the explosion and quick pain in his side, Eddie had walked away. He wasn't sure where he was going, just into the dark of the street where no one could see him.

But he saw the girl around the corner, the one with the sharp mouth who always turned away

258

from his offers, and this time she listened. He asked her to help him, told her he would give her half of his heroin if she would get him to the blockhouse. She'd hesitated at first and then nodded her head. She stayed at his other side, steadied him when he'd started to fall until they'd gotten through the field to the blockhouse where Eddie laid down. Then he'd reached deep into his pocket and came out with the hundred-dollar bill and made her promise to go buy a bundle and bring it back. She took the money and left. He would give her half, he thought, and then he could get himself high and think of what to do.

Now he was thinking about her. Would she come back? Would she just use him like the others? His blood was seeping into the mattress, the stain spreading around him. No, she would come back, he thought. He could hear her outside, stepping through the grass. Eddie would get what he needed. Eddie always got what he needed.

I stayed on the streets, jogging at an even pace down the center, reading the signs at each intersection and recalling the way Richards and I had come the night of our zone tour. I could find the blockhouse again and that gave me an advantage over McCane. I had to figure Eddie Baines would not be armed. If the girl had told the truth he'd tossed the Brown Man's gun. And in not one of the rapes or killings had a gun been used.

I hoped he was injured, but not dead. We needed

him to talk, not to die. If he had killed Billy's women, he could make the case against Marshack. With that we could string the payoff evidence to McCane. With that they could go after the insurance investors. "Not dead," I said out loud.

When I got to Thirteenth Street I saw the open stretch of darkness and recognized the field. There was no spotlight this time, but the night eyes I'd developed on my river would help me find the dull glow of concrete far in the back of the lot.

I tried to move quietly through the high grass but each step was like shaking a half-filled paper bag.

Ten feet away I could hear him breathing, the inhalations like a big, laboring beast but with a low gurgling sound at the end. He was mumbling with each exhalation but I couldn't make out the words.

Three long, careful steps more and the cinder block was cool against my hands. The window was around the corner on the wall to my right, the door around the one on my left.

I moved to the door and crouched for several seconds, listening, and heard him mutter, "She'll come back." I stayed low when I breached the doorway and looked high, thinking of his size. He saw me first from his position down on the mattress but in the dim light his face seemed to hold more disappointment than surprise.

Then he scrambled, digging his heels into the mattress and pushing his way up the wall to gain his feet.

"Easy, Eddie. Easy," I said, standing up with my hands out, palms showing but ready to clinch. "I'm a cop, Eddie. I'm a cop. Nobody's here to hurt you, big man."

He rocked his back against the wall and the dull light from the window next to him glistened on the stain covering his side.

"I knows lots of police," he said in a low mumble, and I could hear a bubbling deep in his throat.

"I know you do, Eddie. I know. You know Dr. Marshack, right? He works with the police."

I could read the recognition in his face, but his eyes quickly covered it.

"I do not know," he said and shifted his left foot forward.

I took a balanced stance. I'd sparred with big men, knew the dip they often took before lunging or throwing a punch, and I watched for it.

"Sure you do, Eddie," I said. "Dr. Harold Marshack, the one who helped you in jail, the one who gives you the money and the names of the old women."

Again his eyes changed and he seemed to start to say something when I saw the dip to the right. I shot out a jab, snapping it into his hand as he reached out to grab me. I pivoted away. He stood his ground.

It was not a boxing ring and far too cramped to dance away. He was not a slow man, despite his size and the bullet wound. When I'd hit his hand hard with my fist it felt like hitting a thick bag of rolled coins, and he hadn't flinched. I couldn't let him get a hold of me. I knew what his hands had already done.

"Come on, Eddie," I tried again. "Why don't we just

settle down here and we'll go talk with Dr. Marshack. You trust him, don't you?"

"I do not know," he repeated.

I was trying to get him to think of something besides crushing me, but I saw him dip again. This time he charged, and I ducked and sidestepped to my right and felt his thick fingers drag across the left side of my neck. He crashed hard against the wall, but then spun.

Now I was in the corner, away from the door and any chance of escape. Jesus, I thought, how smart is this guy? Now I had my fists up, in a boxer's stance. The questioning was over.

He took another, slower swipe with his open left hand and again I punched at it, feeling my fist snap a bone in one of his fingers. He shuffled, but never winced. He was testing me. Watching. Learning.

I took a step to the right, toward the window, and he moved that way, too. I saw him dip and I reacted by sliding to my left, but he had faked me and when my foot lost purchase on a pile of greasy paper he charged. I tried to spin away but he snatched my left forearm in his grip and pulled me to him as his back slammed into the wall. I felt the muscle in my arm flatten and roll under the pressure of his fingers and an electric pain shot up into my shoulder as he tightened the grip and my vision started to spark.

"It was their time," he bellowed and slung me into the opposite wall. "It was their time. Mr. Harold said it was their time." He hesitated with the words, his eyes seeming to blink at their meaning like he'd made a mistake, and it was enough for me to gain my balance. I set my right foot and pounded my free fist into the big man's bloodied side with as much leverage as I could find. This time he winced and a stench of breath popped from his mouth and I landed another blow, and another, and now my eyes were closed and I was back in O'Hara's gym and my father's face was showing his disgust, and I landed another, and another . . .

I was still punching when I felt the presence behind me. When I turned, McCane's girth had filled the doorway. Light caught the brushed metal of the 9mm in his hand.

"Don't stop on account of me, bud," he said.

Eddie lay unconscious in the corner and when I looked down at my hand, his blood was glistening on my fist and up to my forearm.

"Is this what you wanted, McCane?" I said, turning back to the investigator, trying to see his eyes. His face was shrouded in the dark and I could not register his reaction.

"Hell, Freeman. I'm just helpin' you out. Like partners, right?" he said, moving from the doorway to the window and taking a quick look outside. "And it does look like you found our man."

A sound like a low boil in a deep cave came from down in the corner and I felt one of Eddie's boots shift against my pant leg.

"Course, it's not gonna do either of us any good if this boy lives now, is it, Freeman?"

"He said enough already, McCane. Enough to tie

him in with Marshack. And it'll be a short jump to put Marshack with you."

"Yeah, I heard him," McCane said, reaching back into his waist band with his free hand and coming out with a small, tape-handled .38.

"You ever carry a throw-down piece when you worked Philly, Freeman?"

He was looking at the gun, his other hand still flexing on the 9mm at his side.

"Now this little shit piece is just the kind that a boy like this might be carryin'. Just the kind he might use when some P.I. tries to arrest him out here in the dark," he said, waving the short barrel at Eddie.

McCane moved a step forward. His face was dark and I could still not see his eyes, and he could not see the flash of gunmetal come through the window behind him. My recognition started to turn him when the barrel of Richards's Glock found the spot just behind the curve of his ear.

"Freeze it up, asshole!" she yelled.

McCane did not flinch, but only chuckled at the sound of her voice.

"Now, missy. Ya'll sound real tough when you use them movie words. But I don't suspect you ever pulled that trigger on a real man," he said, as he subtly shifted the aim of the .38 from Eddie's chest to mine.

I could see the skin tighten around Richards's eyes and I was just about to warn her of the 9mm still in McCane's other hand when the explosion of noise filled the room and stole the air from my chest.

McCane toppled, stiff-legged, to the floor, his finger

frozen on the trigger of the .38. I stared at the window and could see Richards's gun, extended into the smoke and smell of cordite. She was still sighting down the barrel.

"You don't let anyone point a gun at a fellow cop," she said, her lips beginning to tremble. "That's one of the first things you learn when you're a real officer on the street."

35

Red and blue lights swirled through the trees and headlights crosshatched the open field, and all the sudden attention on the place seemed to make it shrink. A few residents had gathered at a distance in the street.

I sat on the rear bumper of an open ambulance. One paramedic was trying to cradle my arm into a sling while another was using an antiseptic-soaked towel to wipe the blood off the knuckles of my right fist.

Richards was next to me. Her weapon had been taken and placed into a plastic evidence bag for the shooting review board.

We both watched as Eddie Baines was taken from the blockhouse to a waiting ambulance. It took four men to lift him onto a wheeled stretcher and push him through the high grass. Sergeant Carannante said Baines was unconscious when they arrived. A paramedic had guessed the man had lost several pints of blood from the gunshot wound. He doubted he would survive.

Almost apologetically the sergeant explained that the call to the river had been a false alarm, that the man seen pushing a cart had been a late-night janitor wheeling a bin of trash through the alley to a Dumpster.

"There was so much radio traffic, no one recognized your call," he said to Richards. "The dispatcher thought you were with us, and so did I.

"Then it took us a while to get here and we couldn't figure out why Mr. Freeman's truck was parked in the road with a girl handcuffed to the steering wheel."

I looked at Richards and she shook her head.

"Witness," she said. "Oh, by the way. There's a hundred-dollar bill in the locked glove box that needs to be bagged for evidence."

The sergeant nodded, as if nothing this night would be an unusual request.

"And we've got to get you over to administration, Detective," he said to Richards. "Chief Hammonds is waiting. And you don't want to see this."

Across the field the coroner's team was removing McCane's body, hefting the black bag across the dried grass. Richards got up, touched my shoulder and when I looked into her eyes her fingers drifted to the scar on my neck and a single tear stained her cheek. I couldn't lie and tell her it would be alright.

"I'll follow you," I said.

Carannante followed me to my truck, still parked in the middle of the street where Richards had pulled up and come to back me up. The steering wheel was scraped and gouged where the girl had tried to pull herself free from the handcuffs.

"They took her to the lockup on a vagrancy charge," Carannante said. "That's all we can hold her on for now."

"And Carlyle?"

"Couldn't find him. But he'll surface."

I unlocked the glove box and the sergeant handed me an evidence bag into which I slipped the hundred.

"If they match the sequence number to the ones they found in Dr. Marshack's car, you've got a physical link between him and Eddie," I said, handing him the bag.

"I'll take care of it," Carannante said.

I U-turned the truck and had started down the street when I saw them gathered at the next corner. The three-man crew was standing back away from the glare of the squad cars. When my headlights caught them they turned and started the other way. When I pulled up even to them they stopped and the leader looked into my window.

"Y'all a violent people," he said.

I could say nothing in response. He held out his fist and I tapped his knuckles with mine and he shook his head and turned to continue back north to the off-limits.

36

I was sitting balanced in the stern seat of my canoe, my fly-fishing line lying dormant on the brown-green surface of the river. The May sun was on my shoulders and thighs. The sky was a cloudless blue bowl so deep in color it hurt your eyes to stare into it. I pulled the bill of my cap down farther and tried to will a tarpon out of the nearby tangle of red mangrove.

It had been five months since the emergency room doctors had gone to work on Eddie Baines's exploded kidney, transfusing him with several pints of blood and saving his life. He had recuperated enough to be arraigned on a prosecutor's charge of five counts of murder in the deaths of Billy's women.

His public defender had him tested by an independent psychiatrist who reported the man had an IQ of 57 and that his understanding of the charges was such that he could not possibly aid his attorneys in his defense. Eddie was remanded to the forensics unit of the Florida State Prison system in Chattahoochee.

Under the law he will stay incarcerated there until he is deemed competent to stand trial.

It had been two months since we gathered—Richards, Billy and myself—at Billy's apartment to watch an eleven o'clock news report on the issuing of subpoenas to the Delaware-based investor group that had bought the viaticals on Billy's five dead policy-holders.

The cameras caught Billy's profile in the back-ground as federal marshals carted out boxes of records from the firm's twentieth floor offices. Billy had been retained as an advising counsel to the government probe. The investment company's lawyers had already issued a statement that they had no knowledge of the deaths of the five women, denied having ever em-ployed Frank McCane or having ever heard of Dr. Harold Marshack.

"This is a legal and reputable investment business that carries out thousands of viatical transactions in the southeastern United States that benefit the policy-holders in a time of financial need. We categorically deny any knowledge of the abhorrent claims con-tained in the indictment," a lawyer for the group read from a prepared text into a bouquet of news micro-phones.

"We do not know," I'd said, standing at Billy's kitchen counter, sipping a beer.

"They'll know w-when the auditors get done m-matching up the names and dates and amounts that that Miami hacker burned on a CD before McCane had him destroy Marshack's hard drive," Billy said. "It's the a-advantage of b-busting an intrastate scheme—you get the G to follow the money."

And it had been a month since Billy had given me a half-joking ultimatum: He would continue his legal fight against the state's attempt to take over my river shack, if I would get a P.I.'s license and officially work for him. I'd told him I would think about it.

I was still thinking, my line now snaked out on the water like a curved thread of flotsam. I was staring up at the big osprey perched high in the sabal palm above me, his white chest puffed out, his yellow eye seeing everything. Suddenly, the canoe thumped.

"So, can the fish hear when you're talking?" Richards said from her seat at the other end of the canoe. She was wearing a wide-brimmed straw hat, huge sunglasses and a long-sleeved shirt, but her legs were bare and crossed at the ankle.

"No, I don't believe so," I answered the question.

"Then talk to me," she said.

So we talked about movies I hadn't seen, and books she hadn't read, and places neither of us had been, and we sat back and watched the movement of water and soaked in the warm spring sun and let a Florida breeze softly rock us.

Turn the page for an exciting preview of
Jonathon King's powerful new crime novel
featuring Max Freeman

SHADOW MEN

Available now in hardcover from Dutton

The stinging odor in my nose woke me. Or the rising sound of someone calling my name. When I came partially awake I could hear "Mister Freeman! Mister Freeman!" being shouted from a distance, a panic building behind the words. When my eyes cleared, the sight of white smoke curling and thickening in the ceiling made the panic my own. My house was on fire. I rolled out of bed onto one knee and caught a lung full of the acrid smell and coughed it back out. A weak light was making it through the windows and the shouting and the sound of a man splashing.

"Freeman!"

I crawled to the door, staying low, but glancing up in all four directions in search of flames. I pushed the door open and a wave of fresh air hit my face, causing my mouth to involuntarily gasp open and setting my eyes to tear. Down in the canal approach from the river, the park ranger was waist deep in water. He was balancing a fire extinguisher on his shoulder with one hand and using the other to pull and stroke himself forward.

"Freeman! Are you OK?"

I stood with help from the handrail and nodded. My lungs were stinging with each breath but the oxygen was clearing them. The ranger made the dock and hoisted himself up and started up the stairs.

"You all right?"

"Yeah," I said. "Yeah." The second word clearer than the first.

"The fire's on the backside, north corner," he said, pushing my door open wide with his dripping boot. "Maybe we can knock it down from the window ledges."

He pulled the pin on his boat extinguisher and then bent low and started in. I took as deep a breath as I could and followed. The ranger crab-walked across the room to the north window and I broke for the kitchen counter where my own extinguisher was stored.

The ranger had already figured out the inside latch system by the time I got to the east window. Each of us pulled open the hinged mosquito screens and both pushed our heads out. The flames were crawling up the sides of the shack in an odd wave of blue and orange. They licked up over the edge of the roof but there were no eaves in the design to stop them and let them gain heat. This was a good thing. I saw a billow of white chemical spray fan from around the corner and then stepped one leg through the window and straddled the casement. I pulled the pin on my canister and let loose a spray, aiming down at the base of the flames. The fire retreated but then stubbornly reignited. It looked like the tall piling itself was on fire. I leaned farther out to get a better angle and squeezed off another blast.

It may have been ten minutes, maybe thirty. The ranger's extinguisher ran dry before mine, but we had doused all the live flame we could see. When my can was empty, he helped me back in through the window and we both stumbled out the door and down the stairs. Again the wash of fresh air set us both coughing, and when we reached the dock at the bottom the ranger sat with his feet in the water and retched between his knees. I lay down on the opposite side and cupped the river water in my hands and splashed it up into my face and eyes. It was several minutes before either of us could speak.

"You OK, Freeman?"

"OK," I said, realizing I had long forgotten the ranger's name.

"Griggs," he said. "Dan Griggs."

"Thanks, Griggs."

The eastern sky was lightening though the sun was still too low to break through the tree canopy. In time we both sat up, leaning our backs into opposite posts at the end of the dock. I finally took a solid look at the guy. He was a good ten years younger than me, lean with sandy blond hair and skin too fair for his job in the Florida sun. His ranger uniform was soaked up to a dark line across his chest. His leather boots were oozing mud. He was still wearing his belt with a knife scabbard and a flashlight holder.

"You swim out here at dawn often?"

He grinned and shook his head without looking up.

"I'm usually on dawn patrol out on the main river," he said. "I've seen white smoke rising from your stovepipe before, but when I saw it black, I knew something was wrong and motored up here."

"Couldn't get the Whaler in," I stated.

"Had to tie her up and wade in. But I could see the flames even from deep water."

"Guess I picked a bad morning to sleep in."

Griggs still hadn't looked up into my face.

"I figured you were here 'cause I could see that your canoe was gone from the landing."

"I appreciate you looking after me," I said. "The whole place might have gone up if you hadn't been here."

This time Griggs did look over at me. The irony was not lost on him. Several months ago it was Griggs who had to serve papers from the state informing me that the Attorney General's Office was attempting to break the ninety-nine-year lease that Billy held on the old research shack. Until then I'd been left alone and had even befriended the old, longtime ranger whom Griggs had replaced. But there had been a messy business. Blood had been spilled in these waters through a violence that didn't belong in this place. Many people blamed me and it was a point of view I could not argue. It was after that when the state began trying to toss me out. Billy had been fighting the eviction at my request and was keeping them tied up in legal maneuvering ever since.

"I don't suppose you noticed any lightning while you were on dawn patrol?" I said, finally making it to my feet and looking up under the base supports of the shack.

"Nope. And I'm sure you can rule out faulty wiring." He too had gotten to his feet. "But unless you reached out and doused the back wall with kerosene and lit the match yourself, I'd say you got an enemy."

The ranger was pointing to a small slick of rainbow colored water that seemed to be floating independently on the surface of my channel. Some kind of petroleum-based accelerant had spread into the water.

"Whoever they are they don't know much about Dade County pine," he said. " 'Cause it'd take a whole lot more heat than that to do anything more than just scorch that tough old wood."

While Griggs used my canoe to retrieve a camera from his Whaler, I went back inside. There had been no interior damage and even the smoke had mostly cleared, rising up through the ceiling cupola as the design had intended. Still, the place reeked of burnt oil and wood. I closed the screen frames and changed my clothes. I found my cell phone and started to call Billy but put it off. I would need to stay at his place until the shack aired out, but the conversation I anticipated was better off held out of earshot of anyone else. I grabbed my yet unpacked travel bag and rejoined Griggs below.

In the canoe we took a circle around the base of the

shack. The back wall and northeast support pillar were blackened, but there was no apparent structural damage. We pushed up next to the pillar and I used a knife to dig out a scarred piece of wood and put it into a plastic bag. Griggs had been right about the arsonist's ignorance of the pine's resistance, unless his intent was to be more psychological than physically destructive. Maybe someone was more interested in scaring me out than burning me up.

When we finished gawking, we returned to the ranger's boat and tied a line to the canoe for towing. Griggs motored slowly down the narrow upper river, and the sound of his engine sent most of the river animals I would normally see this early in the day into hiding. But just as he cleared the canopy and pushed the throttle up, I caught a glimpse of the long lazy wings of a blue heron, its yellow, sticklike legs not yet folded from its takeoff. I watched it keep time with us and then circle back toward the west and finally disappear into the distance.